Cursed with a poor sense of direction and a propensity to read, **Annie Claydon** spent much of her childhood lost in books. A degree in English Literature followed by a career in computing didn't lead directly to her perfect job—writing romance for Mills & Boon—but she has no regrets in taking the scenic route. She lives in London: a city where getting lost can be a joy.

FESTIVE FLING WITH THE SINGLE DAD

ANNIE CLAYDON

MILLS & BOON

First published in Great Britain 2019
by Mills & Boon, an imprint of HarperCollins*Publishers*
1 London Bridge Street, London, SE1 9GF

Large Print edition 2020

© 2019 Annie Claydon

ISBN: 978-0-263-08557-0

Printed and bound in Great Britain
by CPI Group (UK) Ltd, Croydon, CR0 4YY

To Charlotte
With grateful thanks

CHAPTER ONE

Up close, he looked even more…

More outdoorsy. Taller and blonder and… Just more. A two-day beard covered a square jaw, and his mane of shoulder-length hair was tied at the nape of his neck. His casual shirt and worn jeans gave the impression of an off-duty Norse god, and Flora McNeith resisted the temptation to curtsey. It was slightly over the top as a greeting for a new neighbour.

'Hi. I'm Flora. From next door.' She gestured towards her own cottage, tugging at Dougal's lead in a fruitless attempt to get him to sit down for just one moment. 'Welcome to the village.'

He looked a little taken aback when she thrust the food box, containing half a dozen home-made mince pies into his hands. It might be more than three weeks until Christmas, but the lights of the Christmas tree in the village had already been turned on, and in Flora's book any time after September was a good time for mince pies.

'That's very kind.' His voice was very deep, the kind of tone that befitted the very impressive chest that it came from. And it appeared that whatever kind of deity Aksel Olson was, language and communication weren't part of his remit. He was regarding her silently.

'I work at the Heatherglen Castle Clinic. I hear that your daughter, Mette, is a patient there.' Maybe if she explained herself a little more, she might get a reaction.

Something flickered in his eyes at the mention of his daughter. Reflective and sparkling, like sunshine over a sheet of ice.

'Are you going to be part of Mette's therapy team?'

Right. That put Flora in her place. Apparently that was the only thing that interested Aksel about her.

'No, I'm a physiotherapist. I gather that your daughter is partially sighted...' Flora bit her tongue. That sounded as if everyone was gossiping about him, which was half-true. The whisper that Mette's father was single had gone around like wildfire amongst the female staff at the clinic. Now that Flora had met Aksel, she understood what the excitement was all about.

'You read the memo, then?' Something like humour flashed in his eyes, and Flora breathed a small sigh of relief. Lyle Sinclair must have told him about the memo.

'Yes. I did.' Every time a new patient was admitted a memo went round, introducing the newest member of the clinic's community and asking every member of staff to welcome them. It was just one of the little things that made the clinic very special.

'Would you like to come in for coffee?' Suddenly he stood back from the door.

'Oh!' Aksel's taciturn manner somehow made the words he did say seem more sincere. 'I shouldn't… Dougal and I are just getting used to each other and I haven't dared take him anywhere for coffee yet. I'm afraid he'll get over-excited and do some damage.'

Aksel squatted down on his heels, in front of the ten-week-old brindle puppy, his face impassive.

'Hi, there, Dougal.'

Dougal was nosing around the porch, his tail wagging ferociously. At the sound of his name he looked up at Aksel, his odd ears twitching to attention. He circled the porch, to show off his new red fleece dog coat, and Flora stepped over the trailing lead, trying not to get snagged in it. Then Dougal trotted up to Aksel, nosing at his outstretched hand, and decided almost immediately he'd found a new best buddy. Finally, Aksel smiled, stroking the puppy's head.

'I'm sure we'll manage. Why don't you come in?'

Two whole sentences. And the sudden warmth in his eyes was very hard to resist.

'In that case… Thank you.' Flora stepped into the hallway and Dougal tugged on his lead in delight.

He took her coat, looking around the empty hallway as if it was the first time he'd seen it. There was nowhere to hang it and he walked into the kitchen, draping it neatly over the back of one of the chairs that stood around the table. Flipping open a series of empty cupboards, he found some packets of coffee and a small copper kettle, which seemed to be the only provisions he'd brought with him.

Dougal had recovered from his customary two seconds of shyness over being in a new environment and was tugging at the lead again, clearly having seen the young chocolate-coloured Labrador that was sitting watchfully in a dog basket in the far corner of the kitchen. Flora bent down, trying to calm him, and he started to nuzzle at her legs.

'Kari. *Gi labb.*' In response to Aksel's command, the Labrador rose from its bed, trotting towards them, then sitting down and offering her paw to Flora. Flora took it and Kari then started to go through her own *getting-to-know-you* routine with Dougal.

'She's beautiful.' The Labrador was gentle and impressively well trained. 'This is Mette's assistance dog?'

Aksel nodded. 'Kari's staying with me for a while, until Mette settles in. She's not used to having a dog.'

'Part of the programme, up at the clinic, will be getting Mette used to working with Kari. You'll be taking her there when you visit?'

'Yes. I find that the canine therapy centre has some use for me in the mornings, and I'll spend every afternoon with Mette.'

'It's great that you're here to give her all the support she needs.'

He nodded quietly. 'Mette's sight loss is due to an injury in a car accident. Her mother was driving, and she was killed.'

Flora caught her breath. The rumours hadn't included that tragic detail. 'I'm so sorry. It must be incredibly hard for you both.'

'It is for Mette. Lisle and I hadn't been close for some years.'

All the same, he must feel something... But from the finality in his tone and the hint of blue steel in his eyes, Aksel clearly didn't want to talk about it. She should drop the subject.

Kari had somehow managed to calm Dougal's excitement, and Flora bent down to let him off the lead. But as soon as she did so, Dougal bounded over to Aksel, throwing himself at his ankles. Aksel smiled suddenly, bending towards the little dog, his quiet words and his touch calming him.

'Sorry... I've only had him a couple of days, I'm looking after him for Esme Ross-Wylde.' Aksel must know who Esme was if he was working at the canine therapy centre. Charles and Esme Ross-Wylde were a brother and sister team, Charles running the Heatherglen Castle Clinic, and Esme the canine therapy centre.

'He's a rescue dog and Esme's trying to find him a good home.'

'You can't take him?' Aksel's blue gaze swept up towards her, and Flora almost gasped at its intensity.

'No…no, I'd like to but…' Flora had fallen in love with the puppy almost as soon as she'd seen him. He'd been half-starved and frightened of his own shadow when he'd first been found, but as soon as he'd been given a little care his loving nature had emerged. The strange markings on his shaggy brindle coat and his odd ears had endeared him to Flora even more.

'It wouldn't be fair to leave him alone all day while you were at work.' Aksel's observation was exactly to the point.

'Yes, that's right. I drop him off at the canine therapy centre and they look after him during the day, but that's a temporary arrangement. Dougal's been abandoned once and at the moment he tends to panic whenever he's left alone.'

Aksel nodded. A few quiet words to Kari, that Flora didn't understand, and the Labrador fetched a play ball from her basket, dropping it in front of Dougal. Dougal got the hint and started to push it around the room excitedly, the older dog carefully containing him and helping him play.

Aksel went through the process of searching through the kitchen cupboards again, finding a baking sheet to put the mince pies on and putting them in the oven to warm. The water in the copper kettle had boiled and he took it off the stove, tipping a measure of coffee straight into it. That was new to Flora, and if it fitted exactly with Aksel's aura of a mountain man, it didn't bode too well for the taste of the coffee.

'I hear you're an explorer.' Someone had to do the getting-to-know-you small talk and Flora was pretty sure that wasn't part of Aksel's vocabulary. He raised his eyebrows in reply.

'It said so in the memo.'

'I *used* to be an explorer.' The distinction seemed important to him. 'I'm trained as a vet and that's what I do now.'

'I've never met anyone who *used* to be an explorer before. Where have you been?'

'Most of South America. The Pole….'

Flora shivered. 'The Pole? North or South?'

'Both.'

That explained why she'd seen him setting off from his cottage early this morning,
striding across the road and into the snow-
dappled countryside beyond, with the air of a
man who was just going for a walk. And the
way that Aksel seemed quite comfortable in
an open-necked shirt when the temperature in
the kitchen made Flora feel glad of the warm
sweater she was wearing.

'So you're used to the cold.'

Aksel smiled suddenly. 'Let's go into the sitting room.'

He tipped the coffee from the kettle into two
mugs, opening the oven to take the mince pies
out and leading the way through the hallway
to the sitting room. As he opened the door,
Flora felt warmth envelop her, along with the
scent of pine.

The room was just the same as the kitchen.
Comfortable and yet it seemed that Aksel's
presence here had made no impact on it. Apart
from the mix of wood and pine cones burning
in the hearth, it looked as if he'd added nothing
of his own to the well-furnished rental cottage.

Kari had picked the dog toy up in her mouth,

and Dougal followed her into the room. She lay down on the rug in front of the fire, and the puppy followed suit, his tail thumping on the floor as Kari dropped the toy in front of him.

'He'll be hot in here. I should take his coat off.' Flora couldn't help grimacing as she said the words. Dougal liked the warm dog coat she'd bought for him, and getting him out of it wasn't as easy as it sounded. Perhaps he'd realise that they were in company, and not make so much of a fuss this time.

Sadly not. As soon as he realised Flora's intent, the little dog decided that this was the best of all times for a game of catch-me-if-you-can. When she knelt, trying to persuade him out from under the coffee table, he barked joyously, darting out to take refuge under a chair.

She followed him, shooting Aksel an apologetic glance. His broad grin didn't help. Clearly he found this funny.

'He thinks this is a game. You're just reinforcing that by joining in with him. Come and drink your coffee, he'll come to you soon enough.'

Right. The coffee. Flora had been putting

off the moment when good manners dictated that she'd have to take her first sip. But what Aksel said made sense, and he obviously had some experience in the matter. Flora sat down, reaching for her mug.

'This is…nice.' It *was* nice. Slightly sweeter than she was used to and with clear tones of taste and scent. Not what she'd expected at all.

'It's a light roast. This is a traditional Norwegian method of making it.'

'The easiest way when you're travelling as well.' A good cup of coffee that could be made without the need for filters or machines. Flora took another mouthful, and found that it was even more flavoursome than the first.

'That too. Only I don't travel any more.' He seemed to want to make that point very clear, and Flora thought that she heard regret in his tone. She wanted to ask, but Dougal chose that moment to come trotting out from under the chair to nuzzle at Aksel's legs.

He leaned forward, picking the little dog up and talking quietly to him in Norwegian. Dougal seemed to understand the gist of it, although Flora had no idea what the conversation was about, and Aksel had him out of the dog coat with no fuss or resistance.

'That works.' She shot Aksel a smile and he nodded, lifting Dougal down from his lap so that he could join Kari by the fire.

'You're not from Scotland, are you?' He gave a half-smile in response to Flora's querying look. 'Your accent sounds more English.'

He had a good ear. Aksel's English was very good, but not many people could distinguish between accents in a second language.

'My father's a diplomat, and I went to an English school in Italy. But both my parents are Scots, my dad comes from one of the villages a few miles from here. Cluchlochry feels like home.'

He nodded. 'Tell me about the clinic.'

'Surely Dr Sinclair's told you all you need to know...'

'Yes, he has.' Aksel shot her a thoughtful look, and Flora nodded. Of course he wanted to talk about the place that was going to be Mette's home for the next six weeks. Aksel might be nice to look at—strike that, the man was downright gorgeous—but in truth the clinic was about all they had in common.

* * *

The first thing that Aksel had noticed about Flora was her red coat, standing out in the feeble light of a cold Saturday morning. The second, third and fourth things had come in rapid and breathtaking succession. Her fair hair, which curled around her face. The warmth in her honey-brown eyes. Her smile. The feeling in the pit of his stomach told him that he liked her smile, very much.

It was more than enough to convince Aksel to keep his distance. He'd always thought that dating a woman should be considered a privilege, and it was one that he'd now lost. Lisle had made it very clear that he wasn't worthy of it, by not even telling him that they'd conceived a child together. And now that he *had* found out about his daughter, Mette was his one and only priority.

But when he'd realised that Flora worked at the clinic, keeping his distance took on a new perspective. He should forget about the insistent craving that her scent awakened, it was just an echo from a past he'd left behind. He'd made up his mind that being a part of the clinic's community was a way to help Mette. And his way into that community had just turned up on his doorstep in the unlikely form of an angel, struggling to control an unruly puppy.

He'd concentrated on making friends with Dougal first, as that was far less challenging than looking into Flora's eyes. And when she'd started to talk about the work of the children's unit of the clinic, he'd concentrated on how that would help his daughter. *His daughter.* Aksel still couldn't even think the words without having to remind himself that he really did have a daughter.

'I've arranged with Dr Sinclair that Mette will be staying at the clinic full time for the first week, to give her a chance to settle in. After that, she'll be spending time at the weekend and several nights a week here, with me.'

'Oh. I see.' Flora's eyebrows shot up in surprise.

Aksel knew that the arrangement was out of the ordinary. Dr Sinclair had explained to him that most residents benefited from the immersive experience that the clinic offered, but he'd listened carefully to Aksel's concerns about being separated from Mette. The sensitive way that the issue had been handled was one of the reasons that Aksel had chosen the Heatherglen Castle Clinic.

Flora was clearly wondering why Mette was being treated differently from other patients, but she didn't ask. Aksel added that to the ever-growing list of things he liked about her. She trusted the people she worked with, and was too professional to second-guess their decisions.

'Mette and I are still working on...things...' *He* was the one who needed to do the work. He was still practically a stranger to Mette, and he had to work to prove that she could trust him, and that he'd always be there for her.

'Well, I'm sure that whatever you and Dr Sinclair have agreed is best.' She drained her cup and set it down on the small table next to her chair. 'I'm going to the clinic to catch up on a few things this afternoon. Would you mind if I dropped in to see her, just to say hello and welcome her?'

'Thank you. That's very kind...' Sudden joy, at the thought of seeing Flora again turned his heartbeat into a reckless, crazy ricochet. 'I'll be going in to see her this afternoon as well.'

'Oh...' Flora shot him an awkward smile, as

if she hadn't expected that eventuality. 'Would you like a lift?'

'Thanks, but Kari needs a walk.' Kari raised her head slightly, directing her melting brown gaze at Aksel. Flora appeared to be taking the excuse at face value, but there was no getting past Kari.

He'd explain. On the way to the clinic, he'd tell Kari about yet another dark place in his heart, the one which made it impossible for Aksel to get too close to Flora. He'd confide his regrets and Kari would listen, the way she always did, without comment.

Dougal had been persuaded to say goodbye to his newfound friends and had followed Flora through the gap in the hedge, back to her own front door. When they were inside, she let him off the lead and he made his usual dash into the kitchen and around the sitting room, just to check that nothing had changed while he'd been away.

She leaned back against the door, resisting the temptation to flip the night latch. Locking Aksel out was all she wanted to do at the moment, but it was too late. He was already giving her that strong, silent look of his. Already striding through her imagination as if he owned it. At the moment, he did.

But if Flora knew anything about relationships, she knew that losing the first battle meant nothing. Aksel might have taken her by surprise, and breached her defences, but she was ready for him now.

Not like Tom... Eighteen, and loving the new challenges of being away from home at university. Her first proper boyfriend. So many firsts...

And then, the final, devastating first time. Flora had gone with Tom to visit his family for a week, and found his parents welcoming and keen to know all about her and her family. But when she'd spoken of her beloved brother, they hadn't listened to anything she'd said about Alec's dry humour, his love of books or how proud Flora was of his tenacious determination to live his life to the full. The only two words they'd heard were 'cystic fibrosis'.

Tom's parents had convinced him that his relationship with Flora must end. She had desperately tried to explain. She might carry the defective gene that caused cystic fibrosis, but she might not and if her children developed the condition then it would be a result of her partner also carrying the gene. Tom had listened impassively.

Then Flora had realised. Tom had already understood that, and so had his parents. Pleading with him to change his mind and take her back would have been a betrayal, of both Alec and herself. She'd gone upstairs and packed her bags, leaving without another word.

'What do you think, Dougal?' The puppy had returned to her side, obviously puzzled that she was still here in the hallway, and probably wondering if she was *ever* going to find her way to the jar in the kitchen that held the dog treats.

No answer. Maybe Dougal had that one right. He'd been abandoned too, and he knew the value of a warm hearth and a little kindness. Flora had found a home here, and she needed nothing else but her work.

'We're going to find you a home too, Dougal. Somewhere really nice with people who love you.' Flora walked into the kitchen, opening the jar of dog treats and giving Dougal one, and then reaching for a bar of chocolate for herself.

Chocolate was a great deal more predictable in the gamut of feel-good experiences. Aksel might be blood-meltingly sexy, and far too beautiful for anyone's peace of mind, but the few fleeting affairs she'd had since the break-up with Tom had shown Flora that desire and mistrust were awkward bedfellows. It was as if a switch had been flipped, and her body had lost its ability to respond. Sex had left her unsatisfied, and she'd given up on it.

If you could trust someone enough...

It was far too big an *if.* She'd kept the reason for her break-up with Tom a secret, knowing that it would hurt Alec and her parents beyond belief. They didn't deserve that, and neither did she. It was better to accept that being alone wasn't so bad and to channel all her energies into her work and being a part of the community here in Cluchlochry.

The next time she saw Aksel, she'd be prepared, and think of him only as a new neighbour and the father of one of the clinic's

patients. When it came to thoughtless pleasure, she had chocolate, which made Aksel
Olson's smile officially redundant.

CHAPTER TWO

AKSEL HAD WALKED the two miles to the clinic, with Kari trotting placidly beside him. It had done nothing to clear his head. Flora's smile still seemed to follow him everywhere, like a fine mist of scent that had been mistakenly sprayed in his direction and clung to his clothes. He was unaware of it for minutes on end, and then suddenly it hit him again. Fleeting and ephemeral, and yet enough to make him catch his breath before the illusion was once again lost.

His feet scrunched on the curved gravel drive. Castle Heatherglen Clinic was a real castle, its weathered stone walls and slate roof blending almost organically with the backdrop of rolling countryside and snow-dappled mountains. The Laird, Charles Ross-Wylde had added a new chapter to its long history and transformed his home into a rehabilitation clinic that offered its patients the best medical care, and welcomed them with a warm heart.

The children's unit was a little less grand than the rest of the building, and the sumptuous accommodation and sweeping staircases had been replaced by bright, comfortable rooms arranged around a well-equipped play area. Aksel had come prepared with a list of things that Mette might like to do, and suitable topics of conversation that might please her. But she seemed restless and bored today, not wanting to sit and listen while he read from her storybooks, and laying aside the toys he presented to her. Aksel's heart ached for all that his daughter had been through.

The awkward silence was broken by a knock at the door. Mette ignored it, and Aksel called for whoever it was to come in. Maybe it was one of the play specialists, who were on duty every day, and who might help him amuse his daughter.

Mette looked up towards the door, an instinctive reaction, even though she couldn't see anything that wasn't within a few feet of her.

'Hi, Mette. My name's Flora. May I come and visit you for a little while?' Flora glanced at Aksel and he wondered whether his relief at seeing her had shown on his face.

'Flora's our neighbour in the village, Mette.' He volunteered the information in English, and Mette displayed no interest. Flora sat down on the floor next to them, close enough for Mette to be able to see her face.

'I work here, at the clinic. I'm a physiotherapist.' Mette's head tilted enquiringly towards Flora at the sound of a word she didn't know. 'That means that I help people who are hurt to feel well again.'

'Where do they hurt…?' Mette frowned.

'All sorts of places. Their arms might hurt, or their legs. Sometimes it's their backs or their hips.'

Mette nodded sagely. She'd grown used to being surrounded by doctors and various other medical specialists, and while Aksel valued their kindness, it wasn't what he wanted for his daughter.

'Have you come to make me better?'

The question almost tore his heart out. No one could make Mette better, and he wondered how Flora could answer a question that left him lost for words.

'No, sweetie. I'm sorry, but I can't make your eyes better.' Flora pulled a sad face, the look in her eyes seeming to match his own feelings exactly. 'You have a doctor of your own to look after you. Dr Sinclair is very important around here, and he only looks after *very* important people...'

Flora leaned forward, imparting the information almost in a whisper, as if it were some kind of secret. She was making it sound as if Mette was someone special, not just a patient or a child who couldn't be helped.

'*I've* come because I heard that you were here, all the way from Norway. I'd like to be friends with you, if that's all right?'

Maybe it was the smile that did it. Aksel wouldn't be all that surprised, he'd already fallen victim to Flora's smile. Mette moved a little closer to her, reaching out as if to feel the warmth of the sun.

'I have a little something that I thought you might like...' Flora produced a carrier bag from behind her back, giving a little shiver of excitement. Mette was hooked now, and she took the bag.

'What is it?' There was something inside, and Mette pulled out a parcel, wrapped in shiny paper that caught the light.

'Open it up and see.'

Mette didn't want to tear the wrappings and Flora waited patiently, guiding her fingers towards the clear tape that held it down. It peeled off easily, and Mette got the paper off in one piece, laying it carefully to one side, and started to inspect her gift.

A rag doll, with a brightly coloured dress and a wide smile stitched onto her face. Mette smiled, clutching the doll tightly to her chest.

'Why don't you show her to your dad?'

'Papa, look.' Mette held out the doll, and Aksel's heart began to thump in his chest. It wasn't the gift that had made Mette smile, but the way it had been given. The way it was wrapped so carefully, and the warmth of Flora's manner.

'It's beautiful… Thank you, Flora.'

'*She's* beautiful, Papa,' Mette corrected him.

'Yes, of course. Sorry. What's her name?'

Mette thought for a moment. 'Annette.' His daughter pronounced the name with a Norwe-

gian inflection and Aksel repeated the English
version for Flora.

'That's a lovely name. It sounds even better
the way you say it...' Flora waited, and Mette
responded, saying the name again so that Flora
could mimic her.

This was all so easy, suddenly. Mette laughed
over the way that Flora struggled to get her
tongue around the Norwegian pronunciation,
and when Flora stretched out her arms Mette
gave her a hug. So simple, so natural, without
any of the thought that Aksel put into his hugs.
None of the wondering whether he was going
too fast, or too slowly.

But, then, Flora didn't have agonised hope
to contend with. Or the feeling that he didn't
deserve Mette's hugs. Aksel watched as Mette
showed Flora her toys, noticing that Flora
didn't help Mette as much as he did, and that
his daughter responded to that by becoming
more animated.

'What's that?' Flora pointed to a box of
jumbo-sized dominoes and Mette opened it,
tipping the contents onto the floor. 'Oh, dominoes! I *love* dominoes...'

'Would you like to play?' The words slipped

out before Aksel could stop them. He wanted to watch her with Mette for just a little longer.

Flora treated the request as if it was an invitation to a tour of the seven wonders of the world. Mette couldn't resist her excited smile and gave an emphatic '*Yes*!'

'Shall we do that thing first…?' Mette took a few uncertain steps towards Flora, clearly wanting to know what *that thing* was. Aksel wanted to know too. 'Where you stand them all up in a row and then knock them down again?'

Flora started to gather the dominoes together, putting them in a pile on the floor. 'It's such fun. Your papa will show you, I can never get them to balance properly.'

That was a ruse to get him involved. But Flora could manipulate him as much as she liked if this was the result. Aksel sat down on the floor, and started to line the dominoes up in a spiral pattern, seeing his own hand shake with emotion as he did so. Flora and Mette were both watching him intently, Mette bending forward to see.

'Spirals, eh? Show-off…' Flora murmured the words and Aksel felt his shoulders relax suddenly. Maybe this wasn't so difficult after all.

* * *

When Flora walked out to her car, it was already getting dark. She'd stayed longer than she'd intended with Aksel and Mette, and the work that she'd expected to take an hour had taken two. That might be something to do with the daydreaming. Aksel's bulk and strength and the gentle vulnerability that little blonde-haired, blue-eyed Mette brought out in him were downright mouth-watering.

He was so anxious to please and yet so awkward with his daughter. Aksel watched over Mette's every move, ready to catch her if there was even the smallest likelihood that she might fall. He meant well, but he was smothering her.

Not your business, Flora. Dr Sinclair will deal with it.

Lyle Sinclair had a way of taking patients or their families aside and gently suggesting new ways of looking at things. And Lyle would have the advantage of not feeling quite so hot under the collar at the mere thought of a conversation with Aksel.

'Flora!'

Flora closed her eyes in resignation at the sound of his voice. However hard she tried to escape him… When she turned and saw him striding across the car park towards her, she didn't want to escape him at all.

'I wanted to thank you.'

He'd done that already. More than once, and in as many words as Aksel seemed capable of.

'It was my pleasure. I always bring a little gift for the children, to make them feel welcome.' She'd told him that already, too. They could go on for ever like this, repeating the same things over and over again.

'I…' He spread his hands in a gesture of helplessness. 'You have a way with children.'

He made it sound as if it was some kind of supernatural power. Flora frowned. 'Children are just…people. Only they're usually a bit more fun.'

'You have a way with *people,* then.'

It was a nice compliment, especially since it was accompanied by his smile. Something was bugging him, but she wasn't the right person to speak to about it. She had too much baggage…

Baggage or experience? Experience was something that she could use to help her get things right this time. She'd been an impressionable teenager when she'd loved Tom, but she knew better now. There was no cosmic rule that said she had to fall for Aksel, and she could handle the regrets over never being able to trust a man enough to build a relationship. If that meant that she'd never be able to sit on the floor and play dominoes with her own child, she could deal with that, too.

Flora turned, opening the rear door of her car and dumping her bags in the footwell. Then she faced him. If all he had to throw at her were longing and regret, she'd already made her peace with them, a long time ago.

'You've said "Thank you" already, there's no need for us to stand in the cold here while you say it again. What's bugging you?'

That was obviously confronting. But the slight twitch at the corners of his mouth told Flora that challenge was one of the things that he thrived on.

He took a breath, as if preparing himself. 'My relationship with Mette's mother was over before Mette was born and we never lived together as a family.'

What was he trying to say? That he'd been an absent father who hardly knew his own child?

His obvious commitment to his daughter made that difficult to believe.

'And now?'

'I can't bring her mother back, or her sight. But I'd give anything to make her happy and...' He shrugged. 'It's not working. When I saw you with her this afternoon, I saw how much it wasn't working.'

Flora thought quickly. Aksel needed the kind of professional help that didn't fall within her area of expertise.

'Maybe you should talk to Lyle Sinclair. The clinic has a family counsellor who deals with just these kinds of issues, and Lyle could organise a session for you both.'

He shook his head abruptly. 'Mette's just fine the way she is. I won't put her into counselling just because *I* need to change.'

'Maybe it's not about change, but just getting to know each other better. Kathy uses story-telling a lot in her sessions, to make things fun. I'm sure you have plenty of stories about the places you've been—'

'No.' That sounded like a hard limit. 'That part of my life is over. Mette needs to know that I'll be there for her, always. That I'm not about to leave, and go to places that she can't.'

His heart was in the right place, but his head was way off course, and lost without a map or compass. This was something she *could* help with; Flora had grown up with a brother who hadn't always been able to do the things that she had. When Alec had been ill, she'd learned how to go out into the world, and to bring something back to share with her brother when she got home.

'Who says that you can't go together?' Flora gave an imperious twitch of her finger, indicating that he should follow her, and started to walk.

Flora seemed impatient with him, as if he was stubbornly refusing to see a simple fact that was obvious to her. On one level, Aksel just wanted to see her smile again. But on another, much more urgent level, he reckoned that Flora could be just as annoyed as she liked, if only it meant that she'd tell him what he was doing wrong. The first lesson he needed to learn was how to follow, rather than lead, and he walked beside her silently.

They reached the gravel driveway outside the clinic, and Flora stopped. 'You think that Mette doesn't know what it's like to be an explorer?'

The warmth in her eyes had been replaced by fire. Aksel swallowed down the thought that he liked that fire, and concentrated on the point that Flora seemed about to make.

'You're going to tell me different, aren't you?'

'Just think about it. She can feel the gravel under her feet, and she can hear it scrunch. If she bends down, she can probably see it. She can feel the snow...' Flora broke off, turning her face up towards the flakes that had started to drift down, and one landed on her cheek. Aksel resisted the temptation to brush it away with his finger, and it melted almost immediately.

'But she can't see any of this.' He turned towards the mountains in the distance. He'd give his own sight if Mette could just appreciate the beauty of the world around her.

'Exactly. That's where you come in. She needs someone to explore with her, and tell her about the things she can't see for herself.'

'And if it's upsetting for her?'

'Then you respond to what she's feeling and stop. Just as long as it's Mette who's upset by it, and not you.'

She had a point, and this was a challenge he couldn't resist. Aksel's head was beginning to buzz with ideas. 'Maybe I could take a photograph of them. She might be able to hold that up close and see it.'

'*Now* you're thinking… Speak to Lyle and find out whether he thinks that might work for Mette.' Flora seemed to know that she'd lit a fuse and she wasn't taking cover. She wanted more from him.

'Maybe she'd like to go this way.' He started to walk towards the small, sheltered garden at the side of the property and found that Flora was no longer with him. She was standing still, her hands in her pockets, and one eyebrow raised slightly.

If that was the way she wanted to play it. Aksel returned to her side, holding out his arm. 'I'm going to have to guide her there, of course.'

She nodded, slipping her hand into the crook of his elbow. A frisson of excitement accompanied the feel of her falling into step beside him, and Aksel turned his mind to describing the things around them. The darkening bulk of the stone built castle. The sky, still red from the setting sun, and the clouds off to the east, which promised more snow for tonight.

She slipped so easily into a child-like wonder at the things around her. Aksel was considering asking Flora if she might accompany him and Mette when they set out on their own voyage of exploration, but he guessed what her answer might be.

No. You have to do it yourself.

'Careful…!' He'd seen her reach for a rose bush to one side of the path, and Aksel automatically caught her hand, pulling it away. 'It has thorns.'

Something that had been simmering deep beneath the surface began to swell, almost engulfing him. The thought of rose petals, wet with summer rain and vainly attempting to rival the softness of Flora's cheeks, made him shiver.

'All roses do.' She turned her gaze onto him, and Aksel saw a sudden sadness, quickly hidden. 'Will you let Mette miss the rose because of its thorns?'

That was a hard thought to contemplate. Aksel guided her hand, so that her fingers could brush the leaves. 'You must be gentle. In the summer, the rose is the softest of blooms, but the thorns will still hurt you.'

He let her fingers explore the leaves and then the stem, touching the thorns carefully. It seemed to him that the thorns of this world had done Flora some damage, but that she still chose to see roses. She had room in her heart for both Mette and for Dougal, and yet she lived alone. He wanted to ask why, but he didn't dare.

Flora looked up at him suddenly. 'What's next for us to explore, then?'

A whole spectrum of senses and experiences, none of which involved asking personal questions. Aksel took her to the trunk of an old tree, which twisted against the castle wall, and she followed the rough curves of its bark with her fingers. He explained the eerie wail of a fox, drifting towards them from somewhere beyond his own range of vision. The temptation to draw her closer, and let his body shelter her against the wind, hammered against him.

'I can hear water...' Flora seemed intent on playing this game out.

'Over here.' A small stream trickled past the flower beds, curving its way out into the surrounding countryside. Flora's excitement seemed real, and he wondered whether she was play-acting or not.

'I don't think I can get across...' Mette wouldn't be able to jump to the other side, so neither could Flora.

The temptation was just too great. He could justify it by saying that this was what he would have done with Mette, or he could just give in to it and enjoy. Right now, the urge to just enjoy was thundering in his veins.

'I could carry you.' He called her bluff, wondering who'd be the first to blink.

'You're sure you won't drop me?'

He was about to tell her that he'd carried heavier weights, over much more difficult terrain, and then he realised that Flora was looking him up and down. This was a challenge that he couldn't back off from.

'Let's find out.' He wound his arm around her back, waiting for her to respond, and Flora linked her hands behind his neck. Then he picked her up in his arms.

Stepping across the narrow stream was nothing. Having her close was everything, a dizzying, heady sensation that made Aksel forget about anything else. Her scent invaded his senses and all he wanted to do was hold Flora for as long as she'd allow it.

He wondered if she could feel the resonance of his heart pounding against his ribs. Feeling her arms tighten around him, he looked into her face and suddenly he was lost. Her gaze met his, seeming to understand everything, all of his hope and fears and his many, many uncertainties. He might be struggling to keep his head above water, but she was the rock that he clung to.

None of that mattered. Her eyes were dark in the twilight, her lips slightly parted. The only thing that Aksel could think about was how her kiss might taste.

He resisted. It seemed that Flora was too. This was all wrong, but he couldn't make a move to stop it.

'Are you going to put me down now?' She murmured the words, still holding him tight in the spell of her gaze. Aksel moved automatically, setting her back on her feet, and for a moment he saw disappointment in her eyes. Then she smiled.

'Where shall we go next?'

Their voyage of exploration wasn't over. And Aksel had discovered one, basic truth. That he must navigate carefully between the dangerous waters of Flora's eyes, and the absolute need to do his best for Mette.

'Over there.' Light was pooling around a glazed door, which led back into the castle. He needed that light, in order to forget the way that shadows had caressed Flora's face, in a way that he never could.

CHAPTER THREE

FLORA OPENED HER EYES. Sunday morning. A time to relax and think about nothing.

Nothing wasn't going to work. That was when Aksel invaded her thoughts. The night-time dreams of a perfect family, which were usually brushed off so easily when she woke, had been fleshed out with faces. Aksel had been there, and her children had their father's ice-blue eyes. The image had made her heart ache.

And she'd come so close yesterday. Almost done it…

Almost didn't matter. She hadn't kissed him and she wasn't going to. She'd flirted a bit—Flora could admit to that. They'd shared a moment, it was impossible to deny that either. But they'd drawn back from it, like grown-up, thinking people. It took trust to make a relationship, and that was the one thing that Flora couldn't feel any more.

She got out of bed, wrapping her warm dressing gown around her and opening the curtains. Not picturing Aksel at all. Actually, she didn't need to imagine he was there, because he was the first thing she saw when she looked out over the land that bordered the village. Kari was racing to fetch a ball that he'd just flung into the air, and he turned, as if aware of her gaze on him. Seeing her at the window, he waved.

Great. Not only was he intruding into her dreams, he seemed to have taken over her waking moments now. Flora waved back, turning from the window.

Somehow, Aksel managed to follow her into the shower. Wet-haired, with rivulets of water trickling over his chest. Then downstairs, as butter melted on her toast, he was standing by the stove, making coffee in that little copper kettle of his.

'If he's going to stalk me, then perhaps he should do the washing-up...' Dougal was busy demolishing the contents of his bowl, and gave Flora's comment the disregard that it deserved. Aksel wasn't stalking her. She was doing this all by herself.

The doorbell rang and Dougal rushed out into the hallway, knocking over his water bowl in the process. He was pawing at the front door, barking excitedly, and Flora bent down to pick him up. Then she saw Aksel's dark shadow on the other side of the obscured glass. She jumped back, yelping in surprise, and the shadow suddenly seemed to back away too.

She opened the door, trying to compose herself. At least the real Aksel bothered to wait on the doorstep and didn't just waltz in as if he owned the place.

'Is this too early…?' Today he was clean-shaven, with just the top half of his hair caught back, leaving the rest to flow around his shoulders. How on earth did he get such gorgeous hair to look so masculine? Flora dismissed the question for later, and concentrated on the one he'd asked.

'No. Not at all.' A cold wind was whipping through into the house, and Flora stood back from the door. 'Come in.'

She led the way through to the kitchen, and both he and Kari stepped neatly around the puddle of spilt water from Dougal's bowl. He insisted that he didn't want coffee, and that she should sit down and have her breakfast while he cleared up the mess. Flora sat, taking a gulp from her mug while he fetched a cloth and wiped up the water, washing the bowl in the sink before refilling it for Dougal.

'I assume you didn't just pop in to wipe my kitchen floor for me?' Who knew that a man could look sexy doing housework? If she wasn't very careful, she would find herself fantasising about that, too.

'No. I came to ask you a favour.'

'Fire away.' Flora waved him to a seat, and picked up her toast.

'I did some reorganisation this morning, to prepare for when Mette comes back to the cottage to stay with me.' He frowned, clearly not very pleased with the results. 'I wondered if you might take a look, and tell me what you think? I won't keep you long.'

This was where the fantasy stopped. Mette was a patient at the clinic, and Aksel was a father in need of some help. It was safer, more comfortable ground, even if it was less thrilling. Flora got to her feet.

'Okay. Let's have a look.'

* * *

Aksel picked Dougal up in his arms, and all four of them squeezed through the hole in the hedge, Flora shivering as the wind tugged at her sweater. Dougal followed Kari into the sitting room, and He led the way up the stairs. Flora was surprised when he opened the door to the left because this cottage was the mirror image of hers, with the smaller bedroom and a bathroom to the right. She followed him inside.

Aksel had obviously made an effort. There was a toy box with a row of cuddly animals lined up on the top. A single bed stood at the other end of the room with the wardrobe and chest of drawers.

'This is nice. I can see you've covered all the health and safety aspects.' The room was immaculately tidy, which would help Mette find what she wanted. He'd obviously been thinking about trip hazards and sharp edges, and all of the wall sockets had protectors fitted.

'That's easy enough.' Aksel was looking around the room with a dissatisfied gaze. 'It's not very pretty, though, is it?'

It was a bit stark. But that could be fixed easily. 'Why did you choose this room for Mette?'

'It's the biggest.'

'Big isn't always best. In a very large room like this, Mette might find it difficult to orientate herself.'

Aksel thought for a moment, and then nodded, striding across the hallway and opening the door of the other bedroom. Inside, Flora could see a large double bed, which must have come from the main bedroom. This room too was scrupulously tidy, as if Aksel had decided to camp here for the night and would be moving on soon.

He looked around, assessing her suggestion. 'I think you're right. I'll move everything back the way it was.'

'Would you like a hand?' The heavy bedframe must have been a bit of a struggle.

'Thanks, but I'll manage. What else?'

'Well… I'm no expert…'

'Give me your next-door-neighbour opinion.' His smile sliced through all of Flora's resolutions not to interfere too much and she puffed out a breath, looking around.

'You're not here for long so you don't want to make any permanent changes. But it would be great to be able to change the tone and brightness of the light in here to suit her needs. Maybe get some lamps with programmable bulbs that you can take with you when you go?'

He nodded. 'That's a great idea. What else?'

'Taking her toy box downstairs and just having a few cuddly toys up here for bedtime might get her used to the idea that upstairs is for sleeping. If you use bright colours that she can see, it'll help guide her around the room. And what about some textures, a comforter or a bedspread...?'

He walked across to the nightstand next to his bed, picking up a notebook and flipping it open. 'Lights...' He scribbled a note. 'Colours... Textures... Bedspread.'

Flora nodded. 'If you got her a nice bedspread, then perhaps she could use it here and on her bed at the clinic. Then, if she wakes up in the night, she'll have something that feels familiar right there.'

Aksel nodded, scribbling another entry in the notebook. 'Good idea. Anything else?'

'What does Mette like?'

That seemed the hardest question of all to answer. 'Um... Sparkly things, mostly. And she likes it when I read to her. She always wants the same stories over and over again.'

'The ones her mother read to her?'

'Yes. I think they help her to feel more secure.'

'Then use them as a guide. Maybe choose some things that feature in her favourite stories.'

'That's a great idea, thank you.' He made another note in his notebook before putting it into the back pocket of his jeans and striding back to the main bedroom. 'I'll take the toy box downstairs now. If you could suggest a place for it...'

He was trying so hard. Maybe that was the problem, he wanted to make everything perfect for Mette and couldn't be satisfied with anything less. Flora watched as he cleared the cuddly animals from the top of the toy box, trying not to notice how small they looked in his large, gentle hands.

'Oh...wait, I'll give you a hand...' Aksel had lifted the large wooden box alone, hardly seeming to notice its weight.

'That's all right. If you'll just stand aside.'

She could do that. Flora jumped out of his

way, noticing the flex of muscle beneath his shirt as he manoeuvred the box through the doorway. She followed him as he carried it downstairs, swallowing down the lump in her throat. Aksel's strong frame was impressive when he was at rest, but in action it was stunning.

'Over there, maybe...?' He was standing in the centre of the sitting room, looking around with a perplexed look on his face. Flora shifted one of the chairs that stood around the fireside, and he finally put the box down, one hand rubbing his shoulder as he straightened up.

'Is your shoulder all right?' He raised an eyebrow, and Flora felt herself redden. Okay, so she'd been looking at his shoulders. 'Professional interest. I'm a physiotherapist, remember?'

'It's fine. It was just a little stiff this morning.'

His tone told Flora to leave it, so she did. 'Maybe we could move one of the lights so that when Mette opens the box she can see inside better.'

Suddenly Aksel grinned. 'Kari...'

The dog raised her head, moving from relaxed fireside mode to work mode immediately. In response to a command in Norwegian, she trotted over to the box and inserted her paw into a semi-circular hole cut into the side, under the lid. Flora heard a click and the lid swung open smoothly, its motion clearly controlled by a counterbalance mechanism.

The ease of opening was just the beginning. As the box opened, light flooded the inside of the box, and Flora could see that there were small LEDs around the edge, shaded at the top so that they would shine downwards and not dazzle Mette. The contents were carefully arranged in plastic baskets, so that she would be able to find whatever she wanted.

'That's fantastic! Wherever did you get this?'

'I made it. There was nothing on the market that quite suited Mette's needs.' Aksel was clearly pleased with Flora's approval.

She knelt down beside the box, inspecting it carefully. The lid opened easily enough for a child…or a dog…to lift it and the counterbalance mechanism meant that once open there was no danger of it slamming shut on small fingers. The lights came on when the lid opened and flicked off again as it closed, and they illuminated the contents of the box in a soft, clear light.

And the box itself was a masterpiece, made of wooden panels that were smooth and warm to the touch. It was quite plain but that was part of its beauty. The timber had obviously been carefully chosen and its swirling grain made this piece one of a kind.

'Mette must love it.' It was a gift that only a loving and thoughtful father could have made. And someone who was a skilled craftsman as well.

He nodded, looking around the room restlessly as if searching for the next thing that needed to be done. Aksel's response to any problem was to act on it, and he was obviously struggling with the things he could do nothing about. No wonder he was carrying some tension in his shoulders.

'We could go and do some shopping, if you wanted. It won't take long to pick out a few things to brighten Mette's bedroom up.'

'Would you mind...?' He was halfway towards the door, obviously ready to turn thought into action as soon as possible, and then stopped himself. 'Perhaps another time. Whenever it's convenient for you.'

Flora allowed herself a smile. 'Now's fine. I'll go and get my coat.'

Aksel had been struggling to get the fantasy out of his head ever since he'd opened his eyes this morning. Rumpled sheets and Flora's cheeks, flushed with sleep.

Yesterday had shown him how easy it would be to slip into loving intimacy with Flora, but her reaction had told him that she didn't want that any more than he did. The word *impossible* usually made his blood fire in his veins at the thought of proving that nothing was impossible, and it had taken Flora's look of quiet certainty to convince him that there was something in this world that truly was impossible.

He could deal with that. If he just concentrated on having her as a friend, and forgot all about wanting her as a lover, then it would be easy. When she returned, wearing a dark green coat with a red scarf, and holding Dougal's dog coat and lead, he ignored the way that the cottage seemed suddenly full of light and warmth again.

'Why don't you leave him here? They'll be fine together.' The puppy was curled up in front of the fire with Kari, and didn't seem disposed to move.

'You think so?' Flora tickled Dougal's head and he squirmed sleepily, snuggling against Kari. 'Yes. I guess they will.'

She drove in much the same way as she held a conversation. Quick and decisive, her eyes fixed firmly on where she was going. Aksel guessed that Flora wasn't much used to watching the world go by, she wanted always to be moving, and he wondered whether she ever took some time out to just sit and feel the world turn beneath her. He guessed not.

For a woman that he'd just decided *not* to be too involved with, he was noticing a great deal about her. Flora wasn't content with the just-crawled-out-of-bed look for a Sunday morning. She'd brushed her hair until it shone and wore a little make-up. More probably than was apparent, it was skilfully applied to make the most of her natural beauty. She wore high-heeled boots with her skinny jeans, and when she moved Aksel caught the scent of something he couldn't place. Clean, with a hint of flowers and slightly musky, it curled around him, beckoning his body to respond.

'So... Mette's never lived with you before?' She asked the question when they'd got out of the winding country lanes and onto the main road.

'No.' Aksel couldn't think of anything to say to describe a situation that was complicated, to say the least.

'Sorry...' She flipped her gaze to him for a moment, and Aksel almost shivered in its warmth. 'I didn't mean to pry.'

'It's all right. It's no secret. Just a little difficult to explain.'

'Ah. I'll leave it there, then.'

Flora lapsed into silence. 'Difficult to explain' didn't appear to daunt her, she seemed the kind of person who could accept almost anything. He imagined that her patients must find it very easy to confide in her. All their hopes and their most secret despair. Suddenly, he wanted to talk.

'I didn't know that I had a daughter until after Mette's mother died.'

Nothing registered in Flora's face, but he saw her fingers grip the steering wheel a little tighter. Maybe she was wondering what kind of man hadn't known about his own daughter. He wouldn't blame her—he frequently tormented himself with that thought.

'That must be...challenging.'

Her answer was just the thing a medical professional would say. Non-judgemental, allowing for the possibility of pain and yet assuming nothing. Aksel wanted more than that, he wanted Flora to judge him. If she found him wanting then it would be nothing he hadn't already accused himself of. And if she found a way to declare him innocent it would mean a great deal to him.

'What do you think?' He asked the question as if it didn't mean much, but felt a quiver deep in the pit of his stomach.

No reaction. But as she changed gear, the car jolted a little, as if it was reflecting her mood.

'I'd find it very difficult.'

Aksel nodded. Clearly Flora wasn't going to be persuaded to give an opinion on the matter and maybe that was wise. Maybe he should let it drop.

'In...lots of ways.' She murmured the words, as if they might blow up in her face. Flora wanted to know more but she wasn't going to ask.

'Lisle and I split up before either of us knew she was pregnant. I was due to go away for a while, I was leading an expedition into the Andes.' Suddenly his courage failed him. 'It's a fascinating place...'

'I'm sure.' Her slight frown told Aksel that she wasn't really interested in one of the largest mountain ranges in the world, its volcanic peaks, the highest navigable lake on the planet or the incredible biodiversity. To her, the wonders of the world were nothing in comparison to the mysteries of the human heart, and she was the kind of woman who trod boldly in that unknown territory.

He took a breath, staring at the road ahead. 'When I got back, I heard that Lisle had gone to Oslo for a new job. I think that the job might have been an excuse...'

Flora gave a little nod. 'It does sound that way.'

There was compassion in her voice. Most people questioned why Lisle should have gone to such lengths to keep her pregnancy a secret from him, but Flora didn't seem disposed to make any judgements yet.

'I never saw her again. The first I knew of Mette's existence was when her parents called me, telling me about the accident.'

'That must have been a shock.'

It had changed his world. Tipped it upside down and focussed every last piece of his attention on the child he'd never known he had. '*Shock* is an understatement.'

She flipped a glance at him, then turned her gaze back onto the road ahead. But in that moment Aksel saw warmth in her eyes and it spurred him on, as if it was the glimmer of an evening campfire at the end of a long road.

'Olaf and Agnetha are good people. They never really agreed with Lisle's decision not to tell me about Mette, although they respected it while she was alive. When she died, they decided that Mette needed to know more than just what Lisle had told her. That she had a father but that he was an adventurer, away exploring the world.'

Flora nodded, her lips forming into a tight line. 'And so you finally got to meet her.'

'Not straight away. Mette was in hospital for

a while. She had no other serious injuries, she was still in her car seat when the rescue services arrived, but one of the front headrests had come loose and hit her in the face. The blow damaged her optic nerves...'

The memory of having to stand outside Mette's room, watching through the glass partition as Agnetha sat with her granddaughter, was still as sharp as a knife. He'd understood the importance of taking things slowly, but reaching out to touch the cool, hard surface of the glass that had separated them had been agony. Aksel gripped his hands together hard to stop them from shaking.

'Olaf and Agnetha were naturally anxious to take things at whatever pace was best for Mette and I was in complete agreement with that. I dropped everything and went to Oslo, but it was two weeks before they made the decision to introduce me to her. They were the longest two weeks of my life.'

'I imagine so. It must have been very hard for them, too.'

'Yes, it was. They knew me from when I'd been seeing Lisle, but they wanted to make sure that I wouldn't hurt Mette any more than she'd already been hurt. Letting me get to know her was a risk.'

'But they took it. Good for them.'

'Not until I'd convinced them that I wouldn't walk in, shower Mette with presents and then leave again. That was why Lisle didn't tell me about her pregnancy. Because I was always leaving...'

Aksel could hear the bitterness in his own voice. The helpless anger that Lisle hadn't known that a child would make all the difference to him. She'd only seen the man who'd wanted to go out and meet the world, and she'd done what she'd felt she had to do in response to that.

'She must have cared a lot about you.'

That was a new idea. Aksel had been more comfortable with the thought that the only emotion he'd engendered in Lisle's heart was dislike. 'What makes you say that?'

'If the thought of you leaving was such an issue to her, then it must have hurt.'

Guilt was never very far from the surface these days, but now it felt as if it was eating him up. 'I didn't think of it that way.'

'You're angry with her? For not telling you about Mette?'

Yes, he was angry. Rage had consumed him, but he'd hidden it for Olaf and Agnetha's sake. And now he hid it for Mette's sake.

'Mette loves her mother. I have to respect that.'

He was caught off balance suddenly as Flora swerved left into the service road that led to a large car park. That was the story of his life at the moment, letting other people take the driving seat and finding himself struggling to cope with the twists and turns in the road. She caught sight of a parking spot, accelerating to get to it before anyone else did, and turned into it. Aksel waited for her to reverse and straighten up, and then realised that the car was already perfectly straight and within the white lines.

'I'd want to scream. I mean, I'd go out and find a place where no one could hear me, and *really* scream. Until I was hoarse.'

So she knew something of the healing nature of the wilderness. Aksel hadn't told anyone why he'd taken the train out of Oslo towards Bergen, or that he'd set out alone in the darkness to trek to the edge of one of the magnificent fjords, roaring his anger and pain out across the water.

'I didn't scream, I yelled. But apart from that, you have it right.'

She gave a soft chuckle, regarding him silently for a moment. 'And then you went back home and read all the manuals? Did your best to be a good father, without any of the training and experience that most men get along the way?'

That was exactly how Aksel felt at times. He'd loved Mette from the first moment he'd seen her. But sometimes he found it hard to communicate with her.

'I've made a career out of dealing with the unexpected.'

Flora smiled and the warmth in the car turned suddenly to sticky heat. If he didn't move now, he was going to fall prey to the insistent urge to reach forward and touch her. Aksel got out of the car, feeling the wind's sharp caress on his face.

Flora grabbed her handbag from the back seat, getting out of the driver's seat, and Aksel took his notebook from his pocket, skimming through the list he'd made. 'I should get some Christmas-tree decorations as well while we're here.'

She turned to him, a look of mock horror on her face. 'You don't have any?'

Aksel shrugged. 'I'm used to moving around a lot. Whenever I'm home for Christmas, I go to my sister's.'

'Perfect. I love buying tree decorations, and if I buy any more I won't be able to fit them on the tree.' She scanned the row of shops that skirted the car park, obviously keen to get on with the task in hand. 'It's a good thing we came today, all the best ones will be gone soon.'

CHAPTER FOUR

IT WAS UNLIKELY that *anything* would be gone from the shops for a while yet. The stores that lined the shopping precinct were full of merchandise for Christmas, and rapidly filling up with people. Flora ignored that self-evident fact. It was never too early for Christmas.

Unlikely as it might be, Aksel seemed slightly lost. As someone who could find his way to both the North and South poles, a few shops should be child's play. But he was looking around as if a deep crevasse had opened up between him and where he wanted to be and he wasn't sure how to navigate it. Flora made for the entrance to the nearest store.

'What sort of decorations did you have in mind?' The in-store Christmas shop shone with lights and glitter, and was already full of shoppers.

'Um… Can I leave myself in your hands?'

Nice thought. Flora would have to make sure

it stayed just a thought. She smiled brightly at him and made for some glass baubles, finding herself pushed up against Aksel in the crush of people.

'These are nice...'

'We'll take them. What about these?' He picked up a packet of twisted glass icicles.

'They're lovely.' Flora dropped a packet for herself into the basket, despite having decided that she already had too many tree decorations.

As they left the shop, Aksel gazed longingly at the entrance to the DIY store, but Flora walked determinedly past it, and he fell into step beside her.

An hour later they'd filled the shopping bags that Flora had brought with her, and Aksel was laden down with them.

He peered over her shoulder as Flora consulted the list he'd torn from his notebook, ticking off what they already had and putting a star next to the more specialised home-support items that the clinic could supply him with. That left the bedspread.

'I saw a shop in the village that sells quilts. They looked nice.' He ventured a suggestion.

'Mary Monroe's quilts are gorgeous. But

they're handmade so they're expensive. You can get a nice bedspread for much less at one of the big stores here…'

Aksel shook his head. 'I liked the look of the place in the village.'

'Right. We'll try that first, then.'

Aksel was shaping up to be the perfect shopping companion, patient and decisive. He didn't need to sit down for coffee every twenty minutes, and he was able to carry any number of bags. Maybe if she thought of him that way, the nagging thump of her heart would subside a little. It was a known fact that women had lovers and shopping companions, and that the two territories never overlapped.

It wasn't easy to hold the line, though. When he loaded the bags into the boot of the car, Flora couldn't help noticing those shoulders. Again. And the fifteen-minute drive back to the village gave her plenty of time to feel the scent of fresh air and pine cones do its work. By the time they drew up outside Village Quilts she felt almost dizzy with desire.

A little more shopping would sort that out. Shopping beat sex every time. And this was the kind of shop where you had to bring all your concentration to bear on the matter in hand. Mary Monroe prided herself on making sure that she was on first-name terms with all her customers, and if they could be persuaded to sit on one of the rickety chairs while she sorted through her entire stock to come up with the perfect quilt, then all the better.

But Aksel wasn't going to be confined to a chair. The introductions were made and he sat down but then sprang to his feet again. 'Let me help you with that, Mary.'

Mary was over a foot shorter than him, slight and grey-haired. But she was agile enough on the ladder that she needed to reach the top shelves, and never accepted help.

'Thank you.' Mary capitulated suddenly. Maybe she'd decided that sixty was a good age to slow down a bit, but she'd never shown any sign of doing so. And when Flora rose from her chair to assist, Mary gave her a stern glare that implied no further help was needed.

Aksel lifted the pile of heavy quilts down from the top shelf and Mary stood back. Maybe she was admiring his shoulders, too.

'Your little girl is partially blind...' Mary surveyed the pile thoughtfully.

'Yes. Something that's textured might be good for her.' Flora decided that this didn't really fall into the category of help, it was just volunteering some information.

'What about a raw-edged quilt?' Mary pulled a couple from the pile, unfolding them. 'You see the raw edges of each piece of fabric are left on the top, and form a pattern.'

The quilts were rich and thick, and each square was surrounded by frayed edges of fabric and padding. Aksel ran his fingers across the surface of one and smiled. 'This will do her very nicely. Do you have something a bit more colourful? Mette can see strong colours better.'

'That pile, up there.' Mary didn't even move, and Aksel lifted the quilts down from the shelf. Flora rose, unfolding some of the quilts.

'This one's beautiful, Mary!' The quilt had twelve square sections, each one appliquéd with flowers. Mary beamed.

'I made that one myself. It's a calendar quilt...'

Flora could see now that the flowers in each square corresponded to a month in the year. December was a group of Christmas trees on snowy white ground, the dark blue sky scattered with stars.

'Not really what you're looking for.' Mary tugged at a raw-edged quilt that was made from fabrics in a variety of reds and greens. 'How about this one?'

Aksel nodded, turning to Flora. 'What do you think.'

'Do you like it?'

'Very much.' He ran his fingers over the quilt, smiling. 'I'll take this one.'

'I have more to show you.' Mary liked her customers to see her full stock before making any decisions, but Aksel's smile and the quick shake of his head convinced her that, in this instance, they didn't need to go through that process.

'I like this one, too.' He turned his attention back to the calendar quilt, examining the different squares. 'These are all Scottish plants and flowers?'

'Yes, that's right. I design my quilts to reflect what I see around me. But this one doesn't have the texture that your daughter might like.'

'It would be something to remind us of our

trip to Scotland. Perhaps I could hang it on the wall in her room. May I take this one too?'

'No, you may not.' Mary put her hands on her hips. 'My quilts are made with love, and that's why they'll keep you warm. They are *not* supposed to be hung on the wall.'

'If I were to promise to keep it in my sitting room? Something to wrap Mette in on cold winter nights and remind us both of the warm welcome we've had here. The raw-edged one will stay on her bed.' Aksel gave Mary an imploring look and she capitulated suddenly.

'That would be quite fine. You're sure you want both?'

Aksel nodded. If Mary could be an unstoppable force at times, she at least knew when she'd come into contact with an immovable object. Something had to give, and she did so cheerfully.

'You'll give this one to your daughter as a present?' She started to fold the raw-edged quilt.

'Yes.'

'I've got some pretty paper in the back that'll do very nicely. I'll just slip it into the bag and you can do the wrapping yourself.' Mary bustled through a door behind the counter, leaving them alone.

'You're sure?' Flora ran her hand over the quilts. They were both lovely, but this was a big expense, and she was feeling a little guilty for suggesting it.

'I'm sure. I'll have a whole house to furnish back in Norway, and these will help make it a home for Mette.'

'You don't have a place there already?'

'I've never been in one place long enough to consider buying a house. Mette and I have been staying with Olaf and Agnetha—their house is familiar to her and they have more than enough room. I've bought a house close by so that we can visit often.'

Flora wanted to hug him. He'd been through a lot, and he was trying so hard to make a success of the new role he'd taken on in life. She watched as Mary reappeared, bearing a large carrier bag for Aksel and taking the card that he produced from his wallet.

They stepped outside into the pale sunshine and started to walk back towards Flora's car.

'I'll give the quilt to Mette tomorrow when you're at the clinic. Will you come and help me?'

'No! It's *your* present. Aren't you going to see her this afternoon?' Flora would have loved to see Mette's face when she opened the quilt, but this was Aksel's moment.

'Yes. I just thought…' He shrugged. 'Maybe it would be more special to her if you were there.'

'It's your present. And you're her father. She can show it to me when I come and visit.' Flora frowned. 'You really haven't had that much time alone with her, have you?'

Aksel cleared his throat awkwardly. 'Almost none. I relied a lot more heavily on Olaf and Agnetha to help me than I realised.'

'And how is Mette ever going to feel safe and secure with you if you can't even give her a present on your own? You've got to get over this feeling that you're not enough for her, Aksel.' Maybe that was a little too direct. But Aksel always seemed to appreciate her candour.

'Point taken. In that case, I don't suppose you have a roll of sticky tape you could lend me?'

'Yes, I have several. You can never have too much sticky tape this close to Christmas.'

He chuckled quietly. 'You'd be happy to celebrate Christmas once a month, wouldn't you?'

Flora thought for a moment. The idea was tempting. 'Christmas is special, and once a year is just fine. It gives me loads of time to look forward to it.'

'There's that. I'm looking forward to my first Christmas with Mette.'

'You're not panicking yet?'

'I'm panicking. I just disguise it well.'

Flora grinned up at him. 'It'll be fine. Better than fine, it'll be brilliant. Christmas at the castle is always lovely.'

'Just your kind of place, then.'

Yes, it was. Cluchlochry was home, and her work at the clinic was stimulating and rewarding. Flora had almost managed to convince herself that she had everything that she wanted. Until Aksel had come along...

She felt in her pocket for her car keys, watching as Aksel stowed the quilts in the back seat with the rest of their shopping. She'd found peace here. An out-of-the-way shelter from the harsh truths of life, where she could ignore the fact that she sometimes felt she was only half living. And Aksel was threatening to destroy that peace and plunge her into a maelstrom of what-ifs and maybes. She wouldn't let him.

Aksel had spent a restless night just a few metres away from her. Even the thick stone wall between Flora's bedroom and his couldn't dull the feeling that anytime now she might burst through, bringing light and laughter. He imagined her in red pyjamas with red lips. And, despite himself, he imagined her out of those red pyjamas as well.

He set out before dawn with Kari, walking to the canine therapy centre, which was situated in the grounds of the Heatherglen Castle Estate. As they trekked past the clinic, Aksel imagined Mette, stirring sleepily under her quilt. She'd loved it, flinging her arms around his neck and kissing him. Each kiss from his little girl was still special, and every time he thought about it, his fingers moved involuntarily to his cheek, feeling the tingle of pleasure.

Esme Ross-Wylde was already in her office, and took him to meet his new charges, dogs of all kinds that were being trained as PAT dogs. For the next few weeks Aksel would be helping Esme out with some of the veterinary duties, and he busied himself reading up on the notes for each dog.

A commotion of barking and voices just before nine o'clock heralded Flora's arrival with Dougal, and Aksel resisted the temptation to walk out of the surgery and say hello. There was a moment of relative peace and then Esme appeared, holding Dougal's lead tightly.

'Flora tells me that Kari's made friends with this wee whirlwind.' She nodded down at Dougal, raising her eyebrows when, on Aksel's command, Kari rose from her corner and trotted over to Dougal. The little dog calmed immediately.

'Yes. He just needs plenty of attention at the moment.'

'I don't suppose you could take him for a while, could you? Give everyone else a bit of peace? He's a great asset when it comes to teaching the dogs to ignore other dogs, but he's getting in the way a bit at the moment.'

Aksel nodded and Esme smiled. 'Thanks. You know that Flora works at the clinic…?' The question seemed to carry with it an ulterior motive.

'Yes, she came to introduce herself on Saturday, and she's been helping me settle in. We went shopping for Mette yesterday.'

Esme chuckled. 'Shopping's one of Flora's greatest talents. Along with physiotherapy, of course.'

'We found everything that we needed.' The idea that yesterday hadn't been particularly special or much out of the ordinary for Flora was suddenly disappointing. It had been special to him, and the look on Mette's face when he'd helped her unwrap her new quilt had been more precious than anything.

'I've no need to make any introductions, then. I've been talking to the manager of a sheltered housing complex near here—her name's Eileen Ross. We're looking at setting up a dog visiting scheme there and I thought that might be something I could hand over to you. Flora visits every week for a physiotherapy clinic, maybe you could go along with her tomorrow and see how the place operates.'

'I'd be very happy to take that on. I've seen a number of these schemes before, and I know that the elderly benefit a great deal from contact with animals.' The tingle of excitement that ran down his spine wasn't solely at the thought of the medical benefits of the visit.

'So I can put this on the ever-growing list of things that you'll take responsibility for while you're here?'

Aksel nodded. He wasn't aware of such a list and wondered whether it was all in Esme's head. She ran a tight ship here at the centre, and he'd already realised that she was committed to exploring new possibilities whenever she could.

'Leave it with me. I'll have a report for you next week.'

'Marvellous. I'll give Flora a call and let her know that's what we're planning. Is an eight-thirty start all right for you?'

'That's fine. Is the sheltered housing complex within walking distance from Cluchlochry?'

Esme chuckled. 'It depends what you call walking distance. I doubt Flora would think so. You don't have a car?'

'No.'

'We have an old SUV that you can use while you're here. It's a bit bashed around and it needs a good clean, but it'll get you from A to B.'

'Thank you, that's very kind. I'll pick it up in the morning if that's okay.'

'Yes, that's fine. I'll leave the keys at Reception for you.'

CHAPTER FIVE

FLORA HAD ALLOWED herself to believe that going to Mette's room at lunchtime, when she knew Aksel would be there, was just a matter of confirming their visit to the sheltered housing complex tomorrow morning. But when she found him carefully threading Mette's fingers into a pair of red and white woollen gloves, the matter slipped her mind. The two of them were obviously planning on going somewhere as Mette was bundled up in a red coat and a hat that matched her gloves, and Aksel had on a weatherproof jacket.

'Hi, Mette.' Flora concentrated on the little girl, giving Aksel a brief smile, before she bent down towards Mette, close enough that she could see her. 'You look nice and warm. Are you going somewhere?'

Mette replied in Norwegian. Her English was good enough to communicate with all the staff here, but sometimes she forgot when she needed to use it.

'English, Mette.' Aksel gave his daughter a fond smile. If there had ever been any doubt about his commitment to the little girl, it was all there in his eyes. 'We're going on an expedition.'

'Papa says there's a river, and we have to jump across it.' Mette volunteered the information, and Flora felt a tingle run down her spine at the thought of the trickle of water, and how she'd crossed it in Aksel's arms.

Aksel flashed her a grin. 'Dr Sinclair thought that your idea was a good one.'

Okay. Flora wondered whether Aksel had shared her other ideas, and hoped that Lyle wouldn't think she'd been interfering. She'd just been trying to help…

'Don't look so alarmed. I told him that I'd asked you for some ideas and that you'd been very kind.' He smiled.

Fair enough. It was disconcerting that he'd been able to gauge her thoughts so easily from her reaction, and she wished that he'd do as everyone else did, and wait for her to voice them. But Aksel was nothing if not honest, and it was probably beyond him not to say what was on his mind.

Before she could think of a suitable answer, Lyle Sinclair appeared in the doorway, holding a flask and a large box of sandwiches. The kitchen staff never missed an opportunity to feed anyone up, and it appeared that Aksel was already on their culinary radar.

'Hello, Mette. You're off to explore with your dad, are you?' He put the sandwiches down and bent towards the little girl, who looked up at him and nodded. Lyle looked around, as if wholly satisfied with the arrangement.

'Are you going too, Flora?'

'Um… No. Probably best to leave them to it.' This was something that Aksel and Mette needed to do alone. And any reminder of the almost-kissing-him incident was to be avoided.

'Yes, of course.' Lyle beamed at her. His quiet, gentle manner was more ebullient than usual, and Flora suspected that had a great deal to do with Cass Bellow's return from the States.

'How is Cass? I haven't seen her yet.'

'She's fine.' Lyle seemed to light up at the mention of her name. 'A little achy still, she was hoping you might have some time to see her in the next couple of days.'

'How about tomorrow afternoon? Would you like me to give her a call?'

'No, that's fine, I'll let her know and get her to call you and arrange a time. In the meantime, I won't keep you. I'll see you later, Mette.' Lyle touched Mette's hand in farewell and swept back out of the room.

'What's going on there?' Aksel had been watching quietly.

'Just a little romance. Actually, quite a lot of it, from what I've heard.' Flora liked Cass a lot, and she was happy for Lyle.

'That's nice.' Aksel's face showed no emotion as he turned his attention back to Mette's gloves, picking up the one she'd discarded on the floor. Clearly he was about as impressed with the idea of romance as Flora was, and that made things a great deal easier between them.

'You're really not going to come with us?' He didn't look up, concentrating on winding Mette's scarf around her neck.

'I'll come and wave you off.' Flora grinned at Mette. 'You've got to have someone wave you goodbye if you're going on an expedition.'

Aksel put the sandwiches into a daypack and made a show of going through its contents with Mette, explaining that the most important part of any expedition was to make sure it was properly provisioned. This particular journey required three glitter pens, a packet of sweets and Mette's rag doll.

Downstairs, Mette solemnly let the receptionist know where they were going and when they'd be back, and that they'd be documenting their journey thoroughly with photographs. Flora accompanied them outside, wrapping her arms around herself against the cold.

'I want to ride, Papa.'

'All right.' Aksel bent down, lifting Mette up and settling her securely on his shoulders, and she squealed with glee. He said something in Norwegian, clearly instructing Mette to hold on tight, and she flung her arms around his head.

He was standing completely still, blinded suddenly. Flora laughed, moving quickly to remove Mette's arms from over his eyes. 'Not like that, sweetheart. Papa can't see.'

'Thanks.' Aksel shot her a slow smile, and it happened again. That gorgeous, slightly dizzy feeling, as if they were the only two people on the planet, and they understood each other completely.

Flora wrenched her gaze away from his, reaching up to pull Mette's hat down firmly over her ears. The little girl chuckled, tapping the top of her father's head in an obvious signal to start walking.

Flora waved them goodbye, calling after them, and Aksel turned so that Mette could wave one last time. She watched them until they disappeared around the corner of the building, two explorers off to test the limits of Mette's world. Maybe Aksel's too.

Aksel had wondered whether Flora might come to say goodnight to Mette when she finished work. His disappointment when she didn't wasn't altogether on behalf of his daughter, however much he tried to convince himself that it was.

They had a connection. It was one of those things that just happened, forged out of nothing between two people who hardly knew each other. He could do nothing about it, but that didn't mean he had to act on it either. The days when he'd had only himself to consider were gone.

The evening ritual of reading Mette a story and then carrying her over to her bed calmed him a little. As he settled her down, cosy and warm under the quilt, he heard a quiet tap on the door and it opened a fraction.

'What are you still doing here?' Flora's working day had finished hours ago, but he couldn't help the little quiver of joy that gripped his heart.

'I've been working late. I just wondered how your expedition went.'

'We went across a big river! And back again.' Mette was suddenly wide awake again. 'Will you come with us next time, Tante Flora?'

Flora blushed, telling Mette that she would. Aksel wondered whether it gave her as much pleasure to hear the little girl call her *Tante* as it did when she called him Papa. He'd decided with Olaf and Agnetha that they wouldn't push her, and that Mette should call him whatever she felt comfortable with, but the first time she'd used Papa, Aksel hadn't been able to hide his tears.

'It means aunt. Don't be embarrassed, she

calls a lot of people *tante* or *onkel*.' Flora's re-
luctance to be seen to be too close to the little
girl in front of Dr Sinclair had been obvious.

'And I was hoping it was just me...' Flora
smiled as if it was a joke, but Aksel saw a flash
of longing in her eyes, which was hidden as
quickly as it had appeared.

'Not usually so quickly.' Aksel tried to take
the thought back, turning to his daughter and
arranging the bedcovers over her again. 'Are
you ready to say goodnight, Mette?'

'I want Tante Flora to say it with me...' Mette
reached for the cabinet by the side of her bed,
carefully running her fingers across its edge.
Aksel bit back the instinct to help her, waiting patiently for her to find what she wanted
by touch. The clinic staff had told him that he
should let her do as much as she could by herself, but each time he had to pause and watch
her struggling to do something that came so
naturally to other children, he felt consumed
with the sadness of all that Mette had lost.

'It's okay...' Flora whispered the words. They
were for him, not Mette, and when he looked at
her, he saw understanding. She could see how
much this hurt, and was enforcing the message

that it was what he must do, to allow Mette to learn how to explore her world.

Not easy. He mouthed the words, and Flora nodded.

'I know. You're doing great.'

Mette had found what she wanted, and she clutched the small electric light in her hand as she snuggled back under the covers. When she tipped it to one side, light glimmered inside the glass, as if a candle had been lit.

She hadn't done that for a few days, and Aksel hadn't pushed the issue, leaving Mette to do as she wanted. Maybe it was Flora's presence, her warmth, that had made Mette think of her mother tonight.

'Say goodnight to Mama.' Mette directed the words at Flora and she glanced questioningly at Aksel.

'Her grandmother gave her this. Mette switches it on when she wants to talk to Lisle and then we pretend to blow out the candle.'

'That's a lovely thing to do.' Flora's smile showed that she understood that this was an honour that Mette usually didn't share with people outside the family.

They each said their goodnights, Mette including Tante Flora in hers. Flora leaned forward, kissing Mette, and then turned, leaving Aksel to kiss his daughter goodnight alone.

She was waiting outside the door, though. The connection, which grew stronger each time he saw her, had told Aksel that she'd be there and it hadn't let him down yet.

'Would you like a lift home?'

Aksel shook his head. 'No. Thanks, but I want to go and have a word with Dr Sinclair. He said he'd still be here.'

'I can wait.'

'I'd prefer to walk. It clears my head.' It also didn't carry with it the temptation to ask Flora into his cottage for a nightcap. By the time he got home, he would have persuaded himself that the light that burned in her porch in the evenings was something that he could resist.

'I think I prefer a head full of clutter to walking in the cold and dark.' She gave him a wry smile and started to walk slowly towards the main staircase.

There was no one around, and they were dawdling companionably along the corridor. He could ask her now...

A sixth sense warned Aksel that he couldn't.

Someone like Flora must have men lining up to ask her out, but she obviously had no partner. No children either. He wanted to ask about the welcome gifts she gave to all the kids at the clinic, and the quickly veiled sadness he'd seen in her eyes. But he didn't have the words, and something told him that even if he did, Flora would shut his enquiries down.

A couple of nurses walked past them, and Flora acknowledged them with a smile. The moment was gone.

'So… You're still okay for eight thirty tomorrow? To visit the housing complex?'

Flora nodded. 'I'll be ready.'

'Esme's offered me the use of one of the therapy centre's vehicles, so I'll drop in there to get the keys first thing and then pick you up.'

'Oh, great. I'll see you then.' She gave him a little wave, making for the main staircase, and Aksel watched her go.

Flora was an enigma. Beautiful and clever, she seemed to live inside a sparkling cocoon of warmth. When she was busy, which seemed to be most of the time, it was entirely believable to suppose that she had everything she wanted.

But he'd seen her with Mette, and he'd seen

the mask slip. Beneath it all was loneliness, and a hint of sadness that he couldn't comprehend. Maybe he saw it because he too was searching for a way forward in life. Or perhaps the connection between them, which he'd given up trying to deny, allowed him to see her more clearly.

But this chance to work together would set his head straight. Aksel had made up his mind that it would banish the thought that Flora could be anything else to him, other than a friend and colleague. And when he made up his mind to do something, he usually succeeded.

CHAPTER SIX

FLORA SAW THE battered SUV draw up outside at ten to eight the following morning. Aksel was early, and she gulped down her coffee, hurrying into the hall to fetch Dougal's lead. But the expected knock on her door didn't come.

When she looked again, she saw Aksel had opened the bonnet of the SUV and was peering at the engine. He made a few adjustments and then started the engine again. It sounded a bit less throaty than it had before.

That was a relief. The therapy centre's SUV had done more miles than anyone cared to count, and although it was reliable it could probably do with a service. Aksel looked at the engine again, wiping something down with a rag from his back pocket and then seemed satisfied, closing the bonnet and switching off the engine. Then he walked up the front path of his cottage, disappearing inside.

Fair enough. He'd said half past eight, and that would give her time to make herself some toast. She put Dougal's lead back in the hall and he gave her a dejected look.

'We'll be going soon, Dougal.' The little dog tipped his head up towards her at the mention of his name and Flora bent to stroke his head.

When she wandered back into the sitting room, still eating the last of her toast, she saw that Aksel was outside again, in the car and that it was rocking slightly as he moved around inside it. Flora put her coat on and Dougal once again sprang to the alert, realising that this time they really were going to go.

'What are you doing?' Flora rapped on the vehicle's window, and Aksel straightened up.

'Just…tidying up a bit. I didn't realise this car was such a mess when I offered you a lift.'

He tucked a cloth and a bottle of spray cleaner under the driver's seat and opened the car door. The scent of kitchen cleaner wafted out, and something about Aksel's manner suggested that he'd really rather not have been caught doing this.

'It sounds as if it's running a lot better.' Flora wondered if she should volunteer her car for the journey, but it seemed ungrateful after he'd spent time on the SUV.

'I made a few adjustments. The spark plugs really need to be replaced, I'll stop and get some if we pass somewhere that sells car parts. They'll be okay for the distance we have to do.'

'I'm sure they will. It's not exactly a trip into the wilderness. And if the SUV breaks down, we can always call the garage.'

He grinned suddenly, as if she'd understood exactly what he was thinking. 'Force of habit. When you're miles away from anywhere, you need a well-maintained vehicle. I'll just go and fetch Kari.'

The dogs were installed on the cushioned area behind the boot divider, amidst a clamour of excited barking from Dougal. Aksel stowed Flora's bag of medical supplies on the back seat, and then gave the passenger door a sharp tug to open it. Flora climbed in, noticing that both the seat and the mat in the footwell were spotlessly clean.

'You didn't need to do all this…'

'You don't want to get your coat dirty.' Aksel looked a little awkward at the suggestion he'd done anything. He closed the passenger door and rounded the front of the vehicle.

All the same, it would have been a nice gesture on anyone's part, and on Aksel's it was all the sweeter. He clearly hadn't given the same attention to his own seat, and Flora leaned over to brush some of the mud off it before he got in.

'Anything I should know about the sheltered housing?' He settled himself into the driver's seat, ignoring the remains of the mud, and twisted the ignition key. The engine started the first time.

'It's a group of thirty double and single units, designed to give elderly people as much independence as possible. Residents have their own front doors, and each unit has a bedroom, a sitting room and a kitchenette. There's a common lounge, and a dining room for those who don't want to cook, and care staff are on hand at all times to give help when needed.'

'And what's your part in all of this?'

'I'm the Tuesday exercise lady. Mondays is chiropody, Wednesdays hairdressing. The mobile library comes on a Thursday, and Friday is shopping list day.'

'And everyone gets a rest at the weekend?'

'Kind of. Saturday is film night, and that can get a bit rowdy.'

He chuckled. 'So you just hold an exercise class?'

'No, I hold one-to-one consultations as well. I have a lady with a frozen shoulder and one who's recovering from a fractured wrist at the moment. And I also hold sessions for family members during the evenings and at weekends to show them how to assist their elderly relatives and help keep them as active as possible. Just a little of the right exercise makes a huge difference.'

'It sounds like a good place.' He manoeuvred into the drive-through entrance of the canine therapy centre and retrieved Dougal's lead from the back seat. 'I'm almost tempted to book myself in for a couple of weeks.'

'You don't strike me as the kind of person who likes a quiet life.'

Aksel shot her a sideways glance, the corners of his mouth quirking down for a moment. 'I'm leaving what I used to be behind. Remember?'

He got out of the car, opening the tailgate and lifting Dougal out, leading him towards the glass sided entrance. Dougal bounded up to the young man at the reception desk, and Aksel gave him a smiling wave. Flora wondered exactly who he was trying to fool. Everything about Aksel suggested movement, the irresistible urge to go from A to B.

'So you're not convinced that Mette will benefit from sharing your experiences?' By the time he'd returned to the car, Flora had phrased the question in her head already so that it didn't sound too confronting.

He chuckled. 'Spare me the tact, Flora. Say what's on your mind.'

'All right. I think you're selling yourself short. And Mette.'

He started the car again. 'It's one thing to take her on pretend expeditions. But I have to change, I can't leave her behind and travel for months at a time.'

'No, of course you can't. But that doesn't mean that have to give up who you are. You can be an explorer who stays home...'

'That's a lot harder than it sounds.'

She could hear the anger in his voice. The loss.

'Is losing yourself really going to help Mette?'

'I don't know. All I know is that who I used to be kept me apart from her for five years. I can't forgive myself for that, and I don't want to be that person any more.'

His lips were set in a hard line and his tone reeked of finality. There was no point in arguing, and maybe she shouldn't be getting so involved with his feelings. She sat back in her seat, watching the reflection of the castle disappear behind them in the rear-view mirror.

It wasn't fair, but Aksel couldn't help being angry. Flora had no right to constantly question his decisions, Mette wasn't her child. If she'd been faced with the same choice that he had, she'd understand.

But he couldn't hold onto his anger for very long, because he suspected that Flora *did* understand. She'd seen his guilt and feeling of inadequacy when faced with the task of bringing up a child. She saw that he loved Mette, too, and that he would do whatever it took to make her happy. And she saw that even though he was ashamed to admit it, he still sometimes regretted the loss of his old life.

In that old life, the one he'd firmly turned

his back on, he would have loved the way that she understood him so well. He would have nurtured the connection, and if it led to something more he would have welcomed it. But now, even the thought of that made him feel as if he was betraying Mette. The anger that he directed at Flora should really be directed at himself.

By the time they drew up outside the modern two-storey building, nestling amongst landscaped gardens, he'd found the ability to smile again. It wasn't difficult when he looked at Flora. She got out of the car, shouldering her heavy bag before he had a chance to take it from her.

'The exercise does me good.' She grinned at him.

'All that weight on one shoulder?' He gave her a look of mock reproach. 'If I were a physiotherapist, I'm sure that I'd have something to say about that.'

She tossed her head. 'Just as well you're not, then. Leave the musculoskeletal issues to me, and I won't give Kari any commands.'

'She won't listen to you anyway, she understands Norwegian.'

'If you're going to be like that…' Flora wrinkled her nose in Aksel's direction, and then directed her attention to Kari. 'Kari, *gi labb.*'

Her pronunciation left a bit to be desired, but Kari got the message. She held out her paw and Flora took it, grimacing a little at the weight of the bag as she bent over. As she patted Kari's head, Aksel caught the strap of the bag, taking it from her.

'If you're going to speak Norwegian to my dog, then all bets are off.' He slung the bag over his shoulder, feeling a stab of pain as he did so. He ignored it, hoping that Flora hadn't noticed.

Inside the building, a woman at a large reception desk greeted Flora, and they signed the visitors' book.

'Here's your list for today. Mr King says that he has a crawling pain in his leg.'

'Okay. I'll take a look at that, then.' Flora seemed undeterred by the description. 'I'll go and see Mrs Crawford first.'

'I think you'll find she's a great deal better. She said that she'd been able to raise her arm enough to brush her hair the other day.' The smiling receptionist was clearly one of those key people in any establishment who knew exactly what was going on with everyone.

'Great. Thanks. My colleague's here for a meeting with Eileen. Is she around?'

'Yes, she's in her office.' The receptionist stood, leaning over the desk. 'Is that your dog? She's gorgeous. May I stroke her?'

'Of course. Her name's Kari.'

'I'll leave you to it…' Flora shot him a smile, and grabbed the strap of her bag from his shoulder. Aksel watched as she walked away from him. Bad sign. If she turned back and he found himself smiling, that would be an even worse sign.

Flora had gone on her way, warmed by the smile that Aksel had given her, but stopped at the lift and looked back. It was impossible not to look back at him, he was so darned easy on the eye. And the way he seemed to be struggling with himself only made him even more intriguing.

Fortunately, Mrs Crawford was waiting to see her, and Flora could turn her thoughts to the improvement in her frozen shoulder. Aksel was still lurking in the part of her brain where he seemed to have taken up permanent residence, but he was quiet for the moment.

'Your shoulder seems much better, Helen, you have a lot more movement in it now. Are you still having to take painkillers to get to sleep?'

Helen leaned forward in her chair, giving her a confiding smile. 'Last night I didn't feel I needed them so I put them in the drawer beside my bed.'

'Right. You do know that you can just tell the carer you don't need them and she'll take them away again?' Flora made a mental note to retrieve the tablets before she left and have them disposed of.

'She'd come all the way up here. And I might need them at some other time. It's *my* medication, but they act as if it's all up to them whether I take it.'

Flora had heard the complaint before. Drugs were carefully overseen and dispensed when needed, and it was one of the things that Helen had been used to making her own decisions about.

'They have to do that, they'll get in all kinds of trouble if they don't store medicines safely and keep a record. Some people here forget whether or not they've taken their medication and takc too much or too little.' *Some people* was vague enough to imply that Flora didn't include Helen in that.

'I suppose so. It's very annoying, though.'

'I know. Give the carers a break, they have to keep to the rules or they'll get into trouble.' Flora appealed to Helen's better nature.

Helen nodded. 'I wouldn't want them to get into trouble over me. They have enough to do and they're very kind.'

'Right, then. I'll write in your notes that the carer is to offer you the painkillers and ask whether you want them or not. Is that okay?' Flora moved round so that Helen could see over her shoulder. She liked to know what was being written about her.

'All right, dear.' Helen tapped the paper with one finger. 'Put that it's up to me whether I take them or not.'

Flora added the note, and Helen nodded in approval. She'd raised four children, and worked in the village pharmacy for thirty years to supplement the family income, and even though her three sons and daughter were determined that she should be well looked after now, she resisted any perceived loss of independence.

'Who's the young man you arrived with? He's very tall.' Helen's living-room window overlooked the drive, and she liked to keep an eye on arrivals and departures.

'That's Aksel Olsen. He's from the canine therapy centre at the castle. They're talking about setting up a dog visiting scheme.'

'To help train the dogs? I could help with that, but I'm not sure that many of the others could.'

'Well, those who can't help might benefit from having the companionship of an animal. Don't you think?'

Helen thought for a moment and nodded. 'Yes, I think they will. Where's he from? His name isn't Scottish.'

'He's Norwegian. The dog understands Norwegian, too. He's trained Kari as an assistance dog for his daughter.'

'He has a daughter? Then he has a wife, too?' Helen was clearly trying to make the question sound innocent.

'No. No wife.'

'Really?' Helen beamed. 'Well, he might be looking for one. And it's about time you found yourself someone nice and had some bairns of your own.'

'I'm happy as I am, Helen. I have everything I want.' The assertion sounded old and tired, as if she was trying to convince herself of something. Flora wondered how many times she'd have to tell herself that before she really believed that Aksel was no exception to the rule she lived by. That there was no exception to the rule. Fear of rejection made the practicalities of falling in love and having a family impossible.

Helen brushed her words aside. 'He's very good looking. And tall. And such a mane of hair, it makes him look rather dashing. I dare say that he'd be able to sweep *someone* off to lots of exciting places.'

'He's actually better looking close up. Blue eyes.' Flora gave in to the weight of the inevitable, and Helen clapped her hands together gleefully.

'I like blue eyes. Mountain blue or ocean blue?'

Flora considered the question. 'I'd say mountain blue. Like ice.'

'Oh, very nice. And is he kind?'

Flora had worked through her list of patients, and when she arrived back in the communal sitting room, she found that Helen had decided to take part in the exercise class today. It was a first, and Flora wondered whether it was an attempt to get a closer look at Aksel's blue eyes and broad shoulders, and make a better assessment of both his kindness and his capacity to sweep a girl off her feet.

'Right, ladies and gentlemen.' Everyone was here and seated in a semi-circle around her, ready for the gentle mobility exercises. 'I brought along a new CD, ballads from the sixties.'

A rumble of approval went round, and Flora slipped the CD into the player. Carefully chosen songs that reflected the right rhythm for the exercises.

'We'll start with our arms. Everyone, apart from Helen, raise your arms. Reach up as high as you can…' Flora demonstrated by raising her own arms in time to the music.

The response was polite rather than enthusiastic, but the music and a little encouragement would warm things up. 'That's lovely, Ella, try the other arm now. Helen, you're sitting this one out... Now gently lower your arms. And up again...'

This time there was a murmur of laughter and the response was a lot more energetic. '*Very* good. Once more.'

A sudden movement from Helen caught her eye, and Flora turned, following the direction of her pointing finger. Everyone was laughing now.

Aksel was leaning in the wide doorway, smiling, looking far more delicious than he had any right to. And in front of him Kari had obligingly raised one paw, lowering it again and raising the other.

Flora put her hands on her hips and walked over to him. Behind her she could hear chatter over the strains of the music.

'You know what this means, don't you?'

Aksel shook his head, flashing her an innocent look.

'There's a spare chair right there, next to

Helen.' She may as well give Helen the chance to look him over in greater detail. 'Go and sit in it.'

'Yes, ma'am.' His eyes flashed with the ice-blue warmth that she'd told Helen about, and Aksel went to sit down. Kari trotted to her side, obviously having decided that she was the star of the show.

'Right. Let's do one more arm raise.' Flora raised her arms again and Kari followed suit, raising one paw. There was more laughter, and everyone reached for the sky.

'Well done, everyone. Aksel, I think you can do a bit better than that next time…'

Flora always kept a careful eye on everyone during her exercise classes to gauge how well they were moving and that no one was overdoing things. And this time Aksel was included in that. His left arm was fully mobile but he wasn't extending his right arm fully upwards, and she guessed that it was still hurting him. His neck seemed a little stiff as well.

Kari was loving all the attention, and when the exercise session was finished she trotted forward, eager to get to know everyone. Flora started to pack up her things, leaving Aksel to lead Kari around the semi-circle and introduce her.

She'd expected that Eileen would be keeping her eye on things, and saw her standing quietly at the doorway.

'What do you think?' Suddenly it mattered to her that the dog visiting scheme was a success. That Aksel should feel useful and accepted here, rather than dwelling on all the things that he felt he'd done wrong.

Eileen nodded. 'The written plan for the scheme was very thorough and I liked the thought behind it. This is the acid test.'

Flora looked around. Kari was in off-duty mode, which meant that she was free to respond to someone other than her handler. She was greeting everyone with an outstretched paw, and receiving smiles and pats in return.

'It looks good to me. Kari certainly made everyone a bit more enthusiastic about the exercises.' Aksel had done his part in that, too. He'd joined in without a murmur, smiling and joking with everyone. His charm had contributed almost as much as Kari's accomplishments.

'It looks *very* good.' Eileen seemed to have already made her decision. 'It might be a while before he's allowed to leave.'

It was a while, and by the time Aksel had torn himself away, promising everyone that he'd return, Flora was looking at her watch. She needed to be back at the clinic for her afternoon sessions.

As soon as he was out of the sitting room, Aksel called Kari to heel, picking up her bag and making purposefully for the reception area. He signalled a hurried goodbye to the receptionist, telling Eileen that he'd be in touch, and managed to insinuate himself between Flora and the front door so that she had no choice but to allow him to open it for her.

'How was your morning?' He gave her a broad smile. 'Did you manage to get to the bottom of Mr King's crawling leg?'

'Uh? Oh…yes, the carers keep telling him that the elastic on his favourite socks is too tight, but he won't listen. I changed them and gave his leg a rub and that fixed the crawling. You seem to have enjoyed yourself.'

'Yes, I did.'

'I see that your shoulder's still bothering you.'

'It's fine. It doesn't hurt.'

Pull the other one. There was a clear imbalance between the way that he was using his right and left arms, and Aksel seemed determined to ignore it. Just as he was determined to ignore everything else he wanted or needed. But she shouldn't push it. The clinic was full of therapists and movement specialists, and if he wanted help he could easily ask for it.

'We'll get straight back…' He dumped her bag on the back seat and started the engine. 'I saw you looking at your watch.'

'Yes, I've got afternoon sessions that I need to get back for. And if we hurry we should be back in time for you to have lunch with Mette.'

He nodded, the sharp crunch of gravel coming from beneath the tyres of the SUV as he accelerated out of the driveway.

CHAPTER SEVEN

FLORA KNEW THAT Aksel was at the clinic that afternoon, but she didn't drop into Mette's room during her break. It was bad enough that her thoughts seemed to be stalking him, without her body following suit.

Cass had come for her physiotherapy session, glowing with a happiness that matched Lyle's exactly. She'd come to the clinic as a patient, after sustaining injuries to her arm and leg during a search-and-rescue assignment. Then she'd met Lyle Sinclair. Sparks had flown, and the two had fallen head over heels in love. Lyle had been inconsolable when Cass had returned home to America, but now she was back in Cluchlochry for good. She'd spent most of the forty-minute physiotherapy session telling Flora about their plans for the future.

'The movement in your leg is a great deal better. I'm really pleased with your improvement.'

Cass sat up, grinning. 'I hardly even think about it now, only when it begins to ache. Lyle says I should still be careful...'

'Well, you don't need me to tell you that he's right, you should be taking care. But being happy helps you to heal, too.'

'Then I'll be better in no time.' Cass slid off the treatment couch, planting her feet on the floor. 'Especially as I have you to help me...'

It had been an easy session. Flora stood at the door to the treatment room, watching Cass's gait as she walked away, and Aksel intruded into her thoughts once again. Cass was so happy, and looking forward to the future, and it showed in the way she moved. Aksel was like a coiled spring, dreading the future. No wonder he had aches and pains. Tension was quite literally tearing him apart.

He might be able to ignore it, but Flora couldn't any more. His shoulder could probably be fixed quite easily at this stage, but if he did nothing it would only get more painful and more difficult to treat. This was what she did best, and if she really wanted to help him, it was the most obvious place to start.

* * *

Aksel drew up outside his cottage, trying not to notice that Flora's porch light was on. He'd decided that he wouldn't seek her out at the clinic this afternoon, and it felt almost saintly to deprive himself of that pleasure.

As he got out of the SUV, opening the tailgate to let Kari out, he saw her door open and Flora marched down the path towards him, her arms wrapped around her body in a futile attempt to shelter herself from the wind. She looked determined and utterly beautiful as she faced him, her cheeks beginning to redden from the cold and small flakes of snow sticking to her hair. Aksel decided that sainthood was overrated.

'The car sounds better than it did this morning.' That was clearly just an opening gambit, and not what she'd come outside to say.

'Yes, I changed the spark plugs.' The SUV's rusty growl had turned into a healthier-sounding purr now. Aksel closed the tailgate and reached into the passenger footwell for his shopping bags, trying not to wince as his shoulder pulled painfully.

'And have you done anything about your shoulder? I'm not taking any excuses this time.'

'In that case…no, I haven't.'

'Come inside.' She motioned towards her cottage with a no-nonsense gesture that no amount of arguing was going to overcome. He hesitated and she frowned.

'If you don't come inside now, I'm going to turn into an icicle. You don't want to have to chip me off the pavement and thaw me out, do you?'

It was obviously meant as a threat, but the idea had a certain appeal. Particularly the thawing-out part. Aksel dismissed the thought, nudging the car door shut, and Kari followed him to Flora's doorstep. When she opened the door, Dougal came hurtling out of the sitting room to greet them.

He watched as she stood in front of the hall mirror, brushing half-melted snowflakes from her shoulders and hair. 'I appreciate the concern, but there's really no need. These things tend to rectify themselves.'

She turned on him suddenly. 'What's the problem, Aksel? You have a stiff shoulder, and

I'm a qualified physiotherapist. Or are you not allowed to have anything wrong with you?'

She was just a little bit too close to the truth and it stung. He wanted to be the one that Mette could rely on completely. Strong and unbreakable. But there was no point in denying any more that his shoulder felt neither of those things at the moment.

'Okay, I…appreciate the offer and… Actually, I would like you to take a look at it if you wouldn't mind. It has been a little painful over the last few days.' He put his shopping bags down, taking a bottle of wine from one. 'Don't suppose you'd like some of this first?'

She rolled her eyes. 'No, I don't suppose I would. I'm not in the habit of drinking while I'm working.'

That put him in his place. But when he walked into the sitting room, he saw that a backless chair was placed in front of the fire. She'd been concerned about him and waiting for him to come home. The thought hit him hard, spreading its warmth through his veins as he sat down.

Suddenly all he wanted was her touch.

* * *

'Take your sweater off and let me have a look.' Flora congratulated herself on how professional her tone sounded. It was exactly how this was going to be.

She stood behind him, gingerly laying her fingers on his shoulder. 'You're very tense...'

Flora was feeling a little tense herself suddenly. The lines of his shoulder felt as strong as they looked, and there was only the thin material of his T-shirt between her fingers and his skin.

'It's been a long day.'

'What happened?'

He turned suddenly and Flora snatched her fingers away, stepping back involuntarily. She couldn't touch him when the smouldering blue ice of his gaze was on her.

'I didn't come here to tell you my troubles.'

'I know. Turn around and tell me anyway.'

He turned back and she continued her examination. There was a moment of silence and she concentrated on visualising the structure and musculature of his shoulder. Suddenly Aksel spoke.

'Dr Sinclair took me through the results of

Mette's latest MRI scan today. It's clear now that there isn't going to be any more improvement in her sight.'

'There was hope that there might be?' Flora pulled the neck of his T-shirt to one side, reaching to run her fingers along his clavicle.

'No, not really. The doctors in Norway told me that her condition was stable now, and there was very little chance of any change. It was unreasonable of me to hold out any hope.'

'But you did anyway, because you're her dad.'

'Yes. I wasn't expecting to come here and cry on your shoulder about it, though.'

'You can't expect muscles to heal when you're this tense, Aksel.'

Flora felt him take a breath, and he seemed to relax a little. As she pressed her thumb on the back of his shoulder he winced. 'It's a little sore there.'

She imagined it was *very* sore. The shoulder must be a lot more painful than he was letting on. 'You have a few small lumps on your collarbone. That's usually a sign that it's been broken recently.'

'Nearly a year ago.'

'And what happened? Did you get some medical treatment when you did it, or were you miles away from the nearest doctor?'

He chuckled. 'No. Actually, I'd gone skiing for the New Year. There was a doctor on hand and he treated it immediately.'

'Good. That seems to have healed well, but the muscles in your shoulders are very tight. I can give you some exercises that will help ease them out.'

'Thanks.' He reached for his sweater.

'I can work the muscles out a bit for you if you'd like. It'll reduce the discomfort.' It was also going to take every ounce of her resolve to stay professional, but she could do that.

'That would be great. Thank you.'

She was just debating whether it would be wise to ask him to remove his T-shirt so that she could see what she was doing a little better when he pulled it over his head. Flora watched spellbound as he took an elastic band from his pocket, twisting his hair up off his shoulders.

His skin was golden, a shade lighter than his hair. Slim hips and a broad, strong chest came as no surprise, but Aksel had to be seen to be believed. He was beautiful, and yet completely unselfconscious.

'Okay. Just relax…' The advice was for herself as well as Aksel. This was just a simple medical massage, which might make him feel a little sore in the morning but would promote healing. And she wanted very badly to heal him.

He could feel the warmth of the fire on his skin. Aksel closed his eyes, trying not to think about her touch. Warm, caressing and… He caught his breath as she concentrated her attention on the spot that hurt most.

'Sorry. I can feel how sore it must be there…'

'It's okay.' He didn't want her to stop. Flora seemed to know all of his sore points, the things that tore at his heart and battered his soul. He wondered whether all of her patients felt the connection that seemed to be flowing through her fingers and spreading out across his skin.

He felt almost as if he was floating. Disengaged from his body and the cares of the day. Just her touch, firm and assured.

'My brother has cystic fibrosis.' She'd been

silent for a while, working out the muscles in his shoulder, and the observation came out of nowhere.

'That's why you became a physiotherapist?'

'It was what made me first think of the idea. Alec's physiotherapist taught him techniques to clear the mucus from his airways, and he benefited a great deal from it.'

'It's a difficult condition to live with, though.' Aksel sensed that Flora had something more to say.

He heard her take a breath. 'I know how badly you want to help Mette, and how helpless you feel. I've been through all that with Alec. You're tying yourself in knots and that shows, here in your shoulder.'

'It's… I can't change how I feel, Flora.'

'I know. I'm not asking you to. Mette's lost a great deal, more than any child should have to. All she has left is you, and you owe it to her to take care of yourself.'

Aksel thought for a moment, trying to get his head around the idea. 'It sounds…as if you have a point to make.'

He heard her laugh quietly, and a shiver ran down his spine. 'My point is that you feel so guilty that your lifestyle kept you from her all those years that you just want to throw it all away. I can understand that, I've felt guilty about going out and doing things when Alec was ill in bed. But my mum used to tell me that if I didn't go, then I couldn't come home again and tell Alec all about it. You can share the things you've done with Mette, too. Don't be afraid to give her the real you.'

'And that'll make my shoulder better?' Flora might just be right.

'Maybe. I think the massage and exercise might help as well.'

She gripped his arm, rotating it carefully, seeming satisfied with the result. Then she handed him his T-shirt and Aksel pulled it over his head. The movement felt easier than it had for days.

'That feels better, thank you. Can we have that glass of wine now?'

She hesitated. 'It's not something I'd usually advise after a physiotherapy session. Water's better in terms of reducing inflammation.'

'Noted. Since I'm going to ignore your advice and have a glass anyway, you can either send me back to my cottage to drink alone, or join me.'

'In that case, I'd say it's my duty to keep an eye on you. I might need to save you from yourself.'

Aksel chuckled, getting to his feet.

The Advent candle burned on the mantelpiece. Another nineteen days to go. Aksel was sitting next to her on the sofa, and although they'd left as much space between them as possible, it still felt as if they might touch. Christmas was coming, and at the moment all that called to mind was mistletoe.

'Tell me about your family.' He sipped his wine, his tone lazy and relaxed now. He'd obviously forgiven her for forcing him to face the facts that he'd been so assiduously ignoring.

'There isn't much to tell. There's the four of us, and we travelled so much when I was a kid that we didn't see much of the rest of the family. Just at holiday time.'

'Where are your parents now?'

'They're in Italy. Dad's going to be retiring in a couple of years, so I'm not sure what will happen then. He always said he wanted to come back to Scotland. But my brother's married and lives in England, and they're trying for a child. I can't see my mum wanting to be too far away from a new grandchild.'

'What does your brother do?'

'He's a university lecturer. He fell in love with English literature when he went to Durham University, and then fell in love with his wife. The cystic fibrosis has slowed him down at times, but it's never stopped him from doing what he wants to do.'

'That's a nice way of putting it. It's what I want for Mette.'

'She can do more than you think. One day maybe she'll be leading you off on a trip around the world.'

The yearning in his face made Flora want to reach out and touch him. 'I'd like that very much.'

'My brother's never compromised…' Flora shrugged. 'It's caused its share of heartache, but we've faced it as a family.'

He nodded. There was never a need to over-explain with Aksel. He understood her and she understood him. That didn't mean they necessarily had to like what the other was saying, but the connection between them meant that neither could disregard it.

'So… You already know what frightens me. What are you afraid of?'

It was such a natural question, but one that was hard to answer. 'I'm afraid that the in vitro fertilisation for my brother and his wife will fail. They can't get pregnant on their own because of the cystic fibrosis. They'll deal with it, if it happens…'

'So that's a fear that you can face.' He was dissatisfied with her reply. 'What about the ones you can't face?'

'I have everything I want.' That must sound as much like an excuse to Aksel as it did to her. She had everything that she dared reach out for, and that was going to have to be enough.

'Having everything you want sounds nice.'

'I have a fireside, and a glass of wine. It'll be Christmas soon…' And Aksel was here. But however much she wanted to add him to the list, she couldn't.

'And…?' He reached out, allowing the tips

of his fingers to touch hers. Her gaze met his and in an exquisite moment of clarity she knew exactly what he was asking.

She wanted to but she couldn't. Flora couldn't bring herself to trust any man enough to give herself to him. And the froth and excitement of a no-strings affair... It seemed great from the outside. But inside, when all the longing turned into disappointment and frustration, it hurt so much more than if it had never happened.

She moved her hand away from his, and he nodded. 'I'm sorry. I forgot all about my patient ethics for a moment.'

Flora couldn't help smiling. 'I thought *I* was the one who was supposed to be professional.'

'Oh, and I can't have ethics? I'm sure there's something in the patients' handbook about respecting your medical professional and not making a pass at them.' He grinned, his eyes dancing with blue fire.

He acknowledged the things that she didn't dare to. And he made it sound as if it was okay to feel something, as long as they both understood that actions didn't automatically follow.

'Fair point. Would it compromise your patient ethics to top up my glass?'

He chuckled. 'I don't think so. I'll do it anyway.'

This was nice. Sitting in front of the fire, drinking wine. Able to voice their thoughts and allow them to slip away. It was the best kind of friendship, and one that she didn't want to lose. Taking things any further would only mess it up.

CHAPTER EIGHT

FLORA HAD UNDERSTOOD his unspoken question, and Aksel had understood her answer. Maybe she'd also understood that in the electric warmth of her touch, he'd got a little carried away.

She wanted to stay friends. That was fine. It was probably the wisest course of action, and it was just as well that one of them had kept their head. Making love with her might well have turned into the kind of explosive need that had no part in his life since he'd found Mette.

Friends was good. It meant that he could seek her out at the clinic the next day and ask her about the trucks that had been arriving on the estate, wondering aloud if she was interested in accompanying him and Mette on another voyage of discovery.

'The Christmas carnival is a bit of a fixture here. They set it up every year. There's usually an ice skating rink.' They were walking across the grass, with Mette between them, each holding one of his daughter's hands so that she didn't fall on the uneven ground.

'I want to skate!' Mette piped up, and Aksel swallowed down the impulse to say no. The clinic was proving as much of a learning experience for him as it was for Mette, and he was beginning to understand that, *Yes, let's make that happen* was the default position.

'That sounds fun.' Flora's answer wasn't unexpected. 'Perhaps you can skate with your papa.'

Okay. He could handle that. Keeping a tight hold on his daughter and guiding her around the edge of the rink. He doubted whether Kari would be all that happy on the ice.

It wasn't hard to orientate themselves as the carnival site was a blaze of light and activity. Most of the attractions were set up, apart from a few finishing touches, and Aksel recognised a few of the clinic staff using their lunch hour to try out the skating rink. The booth for skate hire wasn't open yet, and Mette was mollified with a promise that he would take her skating as soon as it was.

'We could take a look at the maze.' Flora gestured towards a tall hedge, decked with fairy lights, which lay on one side of the carnival booths.

'There's a maze?'

'Yes, it was re-planted a few years ago, using the plans of the original one that stood in the grounds. They decided to put it here so it could be part of the Christmas carnival.'

It looked impressive. Aksel bent down, explaining in Norwegian what a maze was, and Mette started to jump up and down.

'I want to go. I want to go…'

'Let's ask, shall we?' Flora approached a man standing at the entrance, who Aksel recognised by sight as having come from the village. He turned towards Aksel and Mette, waving them towards the entrance.

It was entirely unsurprising that Aksel forged ahead of them into the maze. The paths were slightly narrower than last year, the hedges having grown since then, and they were tall enough that even he couldn't see over the top now. They were all walking blind.

'Where do we go, Papa?'

He stopped, looking around. There was a

dead end in front of them, and paths leading to the right and the left.

'I'm…not sure.'

'Why don't you lead the way, then, Mette? We have to try and see if we can find our way to the centre.'

Aksel shot her a questioning look, and then understanding showed in his face. 'Yes, good idea. Why don't you tell us which way to go?'

He stepped back behind Mette, who stretched out her hand, finding the branches to one side of her. Kari watched over her, walking by her side, as she carefully walked ahead, following the line of the hedge right up to the dead end, and then turning back and to her right.

'I think she's got the right idea.' Flora fell into step beside Aksel, whispering the words to him.

'Will this work? Following the wall to your right…?' he whispered back,

Flora shot him an outraged look. 'Of course it will. We'll get there if we just stay with Mette.'

'Papa…?' Mette hesitated, suddenly unsure of herself.

'It's okay, Mette. Just keep going, we're right behind you.' He reached forward, touching his daughter's shoulder to let her know that he was there, and she nodded, confident again.

Mette led them unerringly to the centre of the maze, where a small six-sided structure built in stone was decked with fairy lights. Kari guided her towards it, and she walked around it until she found the arched doorway.

'We can go inside, Mette.' Aksel was right behind her, patiently waiting for Mette to find her own way, and he'd seen the notice pinned to one side of the arch. 'We can climb to the top of the tower if you want to.'

The tower at the centre of the maze had a curving stone staircase inside, and from the viewing platform at the top it was possible to see the whole maze, the walkways picked out by sparkling fairy lights. Mette might not be able to see them, but she could still climb, and still feel that she was the queen of this particular castle.

Aksel guided her ahead of him, ducking under the arch and letting Mette find the handrail and climb the steps. Flora followed, Kari loping up the steps at her side. The four of them could just squeeze onto the small viewing platform at the top, bounded by crenellated stonework.

'Papa! I found the way!' Mette squealed with excitement, and Aksel lifted her up in his arms.

'*Ja elskling…*' He was hugging the little girl tightly, and he seemed to have tears in his eyes. 'I'm so proud of you, Mette.'

'I'm an explorer too, Papa.'

Aksel seemed to be lost for words. Flora wanted so badly to put her arms around them both, but this was their moment. Mette had used some of the techniques that the clinic was teaching her, and they'd worked for all of them in the maze. And Aksel had found that for all his height and strength, and even though he could see, he'd not known which way to go any more than Mette had.

Flora waited while they savoured their triumph. Then she reached out, touching Mette's hand to catch her attention.

'Are you going to lead us back out again now?'

'She'd better. I don't know the way.' Aksel's voice was thick with emotion still.

Mette regarded him solemnly. 'What if I get lost, Papa?'

'You won't.' He set Mette back down on her feet, turning to guide her carefully down the staircase.

By the time they'd navigated their way out of the maze, the stallholders had almost finished setting up for the opening later on that afternoon, and the proprietor of the village tea shop was pleased to sell them sausage rolls, warm from the small oven on his stall, and made with homemade beef sausagemeat.

They wandered between the lines of stalls, and when Mette had finished eating, Aksel lifted her up onto his shoulders. Then he caught sight of it, stopping suddenly and staring at the open-sided tent.

'What's that?' He couldn't take his eyes off the large blocks of ice under the awning.

'You want to go and have a look? I'll stay here with Mette.' Flora had a feeling that this was something that Aksel would like to explore on his own.

'I...' He turned, but seemed unable to find enough momentum to walk away. Looking back, he nodded. 'Yes. If you don't mind.'

'Of course not. We can go and get some doughnuts to take back with us.'

'I'll be back in a minute.' He lifted Mette down from his shoulders and Flora took her hand, watching as Aksel strode across to the tent. She'd be very surprised if he was back in a minute.

They chose and purchased their doughnuts, and Flora looked back towards the tent to see Aksel deep in conversation with Ted Mackie, the estate manager. Ted was eyeing him up, clearly deciding whether it would be okay to let Aksel loose with a chainsaw. Flora resisted the temptation to run up to Ted, take him by the lapels of his coat, and tell him that if Aksel could be trusted to get to both Poles and back, he could be trusted with power tools. And that he really needed to do something like this.

'What's Papa doing?' Mette was unable to see her father.

'He's right over there, at one of the other stalls. Shall we go and see?' Aksel had taken the pair of work gloves that Ted had proffered, and was passing them from one hand to the other as he talked. He was tempted. Flora could see that he was *very* tempted.

She walked slowly over to the tent, wondering whether that would give Aksel time to give in to the temptation. She could see him checking out the chainsaw and running his hand over one of the large blocks of ice. Ted was nodding in agreement to something he'd said.

'Hi. We've got doughnuts.' Aksel jumped when Flora spoke, too immersed in his conversation to have noticed them approaching. Flora tried hard not to smirk.

'Oh… I suppose…' He handed the gloves back to Ted ruefully. 'I'd really like to give this a go but…'

Ted flashed Flora a glance. 'Shame. It would be good to have something to show people. It would give us a start.'

'I'd like to but…' Aksel turned, masking the regret in his face with a smile. 'We need to get you back to the clinic, Mette. You've got a play date this afternoon.'

One of the well-organised play sessions, which would help Mette to make the most of her limited sight. They were very well supervised, and Mette was already making friends at the clinic. Aksel really wasn't needed.

'If you'd like to stay here, I can take Mette back.'

'We bought you a doughnut, Papa. So you don't get hungry.'

'Thank you.' He grinned down at Mette, taking the paper bag that she was holding out towards him. 'I should come back with you, though.'

Ted had bent down to Mette and took her hand, leading her over to the blocks of ice so that she could run her hand over them to feel the icy coldness beneath her fingertips. Aksel looked about to follow, and Flora caught his sleeve.

'She can do that by herself, Aksel. Ted's looking after her.'

'I know, but...' His forehead creased into a frown. 'I'm crowding her, aren't I?'

'You're spending time with her, so that you can make a relationship. That's great.' Aksel shot her an unconvinced look. 'And, yes, you are crowding her a bit. She's learning how to explore her world.'

'And this is what the therapists at the clinic are teaching her.' He looked over at Mette thoughtfully.

'That's our job, all of us. We may have specific roles, but we all have the same aim.' Everyone who worked here on the estate was a part of that. Ted took the children on nature walks during the summer, and Mrs Renwick, the cook at the castle, held regular cookery classes for both adults and children.

'All the same, Mette's far more important than this…'

'Yes, she is. She's important to all of us, and she's just starting to feel at home at the clinic. She has a play date this afternoon, and she's going to have a great time. You can either interfere with that, or you can stay here and make her something nice.'

He narrowed his eyes. 'Are you just saying that because you know I want to stay?'

'I'm saying this because staying's okay. Mette has other things to do this afternoon.'

Aksel was frowning, now. 'I was rather hoping that she'd learn to need me.'

Flora puffed out an exasperated breath. 'She *does* need you, Aksel. She needs you to be her father, which means you're always there for her. It doesn't mean that you have to follow her around all the time. The whole point of her being here is to learn to be independent.'

Most people would have hummed and hawed about it a bit. But Aksel had the information he needed, and it was typical of him to make his decision and act on it.

'You're killing me. You know that.' He turned on his heel, walking over to Mette.

'Ted says that I can make an ice sculpture. Would you like me to make one for you this afternoon, while Tante Flora takes you back to the castle to play?'

'Yes, Papa!' Mette obviously thought that was a good idea, too.

'Okay. What would you like me to make, then?'

Flora winced. Maybe it would have been better to give Mette some suggestions, rather than allow a child's imagination to run rampant.

'A reindeer. Mama took me to see the reindeer.'

'A reindeer?' Ted chuckled, removing his flat cap to scratch his head. 'That'll be interesting. What do you think, Aksel?'

Aksel shrugged. 'If she wants a reindeer, then... I can do a reindeer.'

'Would you like me to bring Mette back here after I've finished work?' Flora reckoned that Aksel might need a bit of extra time to work out how to sculpt four legs and a pair of antlers.

'Um… Yes. That would be great, thank you.'

'Right.' Flora took Mette's hand. 'Shall we stay and watch Papa get started on your reindeer, Mette, and then we'll go back to the castle.'

Mette nodded, following Flora to a safe distance, while Ted gave Aksel the gloves and a pair of safety glasses. Running him through a few safety rules was probably unnecessary, but Ted was nothing if not thorough, and Aksel listened carefully. Then he turned towards the block of ice that Ted had indicated, standing back for a moment to contemplate his first move, before starting up the chainsaw.

Mette tugged her hat down over her ears in response to the noise. 'What's Papa doing?'

'He's cutting some ice off the top. To make the reindeer's back.'

Aksel had clearly decided to start with the easy part, and was making an incision on one side of the block of ice that ran half way along its length. Then he made a similar incision from the top, freeing a large piece of ice, which he lifted down onto the ground. He switched off the chainsaw, engaging the safety mechanism, and beckoned to Flora and Mette.

'See this big block he's sawn off. It's almost as big as you are.' She kept hold of Mette's hand, letting her feel the size of the block. 'I can't wait to see what it'll be like when we get back.'

'Neither can I,' Ted interjected. He was clearly wondering how Aksel was going to sculpt a pair of antlers too.

'You're *all* killing me...' Aksel muttered the words under his breath, but he was grinning broadly. He was clearly in his element.

He bent down, kissing Mette goodbye and telling her to enjoy her afternoon. Flora took her hand and walked away, knowing that Aksel was watching them go. It wasn't until she'd turned into one of the walkways between the stalls that she heard the chainsaw start up again.

Mette had told everyone about how her papa was using a chainsaw to make her a reindeer out of ice. When Flora arrived back at the children's unit to pick her up, the nursery nurses and some of the children already had their hats and coats on.

'Are we ready, then?' Lyle was wearing a thick windcheater and was clearly intending to join the party. Flora hoped that they wouldn't be disappointed.

'Should we phone Ted first? To see if it's finished?' And possibly to make sure that the reindeer hadn't collapsed and they'd be greeted by an amorphous pile of ice.

Lyle chuckled. 'Aksel called me earlier for some orthopaedic advice.'

'He's hurt himself?' Flora hoped that Aksel hadn't overdone things and damaged his shoulder.

'No, it was more a matter of how thick the reindeer's legs needed to be to support the weight of the body. Interesting equation. I called Ted just now, and he says that it's all going rather well.'

Lyle looked round as Cass entered the room, displaying the sixth sense of a lover who always knew when his partner was nearby.

'I can't wait to see it.' Cass's green eyes

flashed with mischief. 'There's something very sexy about a man using power tools...'

Yes, there was. And there was something almost overwhelmingly sexy about Aksel using power tools. Combine that with large blocks of ice, and it was enough to melt the most frozen heart.

'You think so? I might have to have a go, then.' Lyle raised an eyebrow and Cass laughed.

They all trooped out of the main entrance to the clinic, Mette holding her hand. It was dark now and the lights of the carnival shone brightly ahead of them, people straggling along the path that led down from the castle.

The first evening of the carnival was, as always, well attended. Charles Ross-Wylde was there, fulfilling his duties as Laird and host by greeting everyone and then melting quietly away to leave them to their fun. His sister Esme had brought a couple of the dogs from the canine therapy centre, and was clearly taking the opportunity to make sure that they weren't distracted by the lights and sounds around them.

Mette tugged at Flora's hand, remembering which way they needed to walk to get to the ice sculpture. As they approached, Flora could see Ted adjusting the lights that were placed at the bottom of the sculpture to show it off to its best effect. And Aksel's tall, unmistakeable silhouette standing back a little.

He turned, seeming to sense that they were there, and walked towards them. Shooting Flora a smile, he addressed Mette.

'Would you like to come and see your reindeer?'

'Yes, Papa!'

Flora watched as he led his daughter over to the reindeer, letting her stand close so that she could see the lights reflected in the ice. It was beautiful, standing tall and proud, a full set of antlers on its head. The lights glistened through the ice, making it seem almost alive.

Over the noise of the carnival, Flora could hear Mette's excited chatter. Lyle came to inspect the reindeer and Mette took his hand, pulling him closer to take a look. Aksel stood back, leaving his daughter with Lyle and Cass, and walked over to Flora.

'That is downright amazing.' Flora grinned up at him.

'I had a bit of help. One of the antlers snapped off, and Ted and I had to re-attach it. And Dr Sinclair's anatomical knowledge was invaluable.'

'Yes, I heard about that. I'm a little more interested in *your* anatomy.' Flora frowned. She could have phrased that a little better. Somehow, a perfectly innocent enquiry about his shoulder seemed to have turned into a barely disguised chat-up line.

'My shoulder's fine. If that's what you mean.' The slight quirk of his lips showed that Aksel was quite prepared to call her bluff, and Flora decided to ignore the invitation.

'I'm glad you haven't undone the work I did on it.'

'It might be a bit stiff in the morning...'

Flora returned his smile. 'If it is, I'll be officially reporting you to Lyle for some more orthopaedic advice.' A repetition of last night was probably to be avoided.

'You make that sound like a threat.'

'Don't worry. It is.'

CHAPTER NINE

AKSEL WOKE UP the following morning feeling more refreshed from sleep than he had in a long time. It was a bright, clear day, and although his shoulder was a little sore, it was nothing that a hot shower and some stretching exercises wouldn't banish. He was ready for the day, and the day seemed that much better for the possibility that it might bring another chance to see Flora.

He wasn't disappointed. When he arrived at the clinic, after a morning's work at the therapy centre, he found that Mette was absorbed in a learning game with one of the children's therapy assistants. He kissed his daughter and told her that he wouldn't interrupt, and then wandered aimlessly down to one of the patient sitting rooms.

He saw Flora sitting in one of the wing-backed chairs by the great fireplace, which had been made bright and welcoming with an arrangement of Christmas greenery. He recognised the sandy-haired man in the chair opposite. One of the children's play leaders had told him that this was Andy Wallace and that he didn't much like to be touched, in a broad hint that Aksel should steer Mette clear of him.

Flora was leaning towards Andy, and the two seemed to be deep in conversation. Aksel turned to walk away, but then Flora looked up and beckoned him over.

Andy didn't offer to shake hands when Flora introduced the two men but nodded quietly in Aksel's direction, clearly taking his time to sum him up.

'We're just having tea. Would you like to join us?' Flora smiled at him.

There was no *just* about it. Flora had been talking quietly to Andy, no doubt discussing the next step of what looked like a long road back to full health. Andy's leg was supported by a surgical brace and his eyes seemed haunted. But if Flora thought that it was okay for him to join them, then he trusted her.

'Thank you. Can I get you a refill?' He gestured to the two empty cups on the small table between them.

'Not for me, thanks. Andy?'

Andy proffered his cup, and Aksel carried it over to the side table where coffee and tea were laid out. He put a fresh herbal teabag into Andy's cup and reached for a coffee capsule for himself. Flora leaned forward, saying a few words to Andy, and he nodded. All the same, when Aksel operated the coffee machine, Andy jumped slightly at the noise.

'Where's Mette?' Flora turned to him as he sat down.

'She's…got something going with the play assistants. Apparently I'm surplus to requirements at the moment.' Aksel made a joke of it, but it stung more than he cared to admit.

Flora nodded, smiling at Andy. 'Aksel's not used to that.'

Andy let out a short, barked laugh. 'I can identify with *surplus to requirements.*' He nodded down at his leg, clearly frustrated by his own lack of mobility.

'It's nothing…' The comparison was embarrassing; Andy clearly had life-changing injuries.

'Don't let Flora hear you say that. She has a

keen nose for *nothing.*' Andy gave a wry smile, and Flora grinned back at him.

'Nothing's a code word around here. Meaning something.' Flora's observation sounded like a quiet joke, and Aksel wondered if it was aimed at him or Andy. Probably both of them.

'In that case, it's something. And I'm handling it.' Aksel's smiling retort made both Andy and Flora laugh. He was beginning to like Andy, and Aksel pulled out his phone, flipping to the picture he'd taken yesterday and handing the phone to Andy.

'Oh, she's a bonny wee lass. What's that she's standing next to?'

Flora smiled. 'Ted Mackie has an ice-sculpting stall at the carnival. With chainsaws. Aksel made the mistake of telling Mette that he'd sculpt whatever she wanted for her, and he ended up having to do a reindeer.'

Andy chuckled. 'You made a decent job of it. Why is your daughter here?'

'She was in a car accident, and she's lost most of her sight. Anything that's more than a few feet away from her is just a blur.'

'You've done the best thing for her, bringing her to the clinic. They'll help her make the most of what she has.' Andy's reaction was like a breath of fresh air. Someone who knew the nature of suffering but didn't dwell on it, and who preferred to look at what could be done for Mette, and not express horror at what couldn't be changed.

'Thanks. That's good to hear.'

Flora had leaned back in her chair, seemingly in no hurry to go anywhere. The talk drifted into quiet, getting-to-know-you mode. Andy had been in the army and had travelled a lot, and the two men swapped stories about places they'd both visited. Andy's story about patching up a broken-down SUV from the only materials to hand struck a chord with Aksel, and the two men laughed over it. And Aksel's story about the mystery of the missing coffee supplies made Andy chuckle.

Finally, Flora looked at her watch. 'I hate to break this up, but it's time for your physio now, Andy.' She was clearly pleased with the way things had gone. And Aksel had enjoyed their talk. Andy had a well-developed sense of humour, and he'd led an interesting life.

Andy rolled his eyes. 'Another chance for

you to torment me?' He clearly thought a lot of Flora.

'Yes, that's right. I don't get paid if I can't find something to torment my patients with.' Flora gave Andy a bright smile, helping him to his feet and pulling in front of him the walking frame that stood by the side of his chair.

'I'd like to see the pictures of your expedition to the Andes.' Andy turned to Aksel.

'Sure. I'll bring them in tomorrow. Is it okay for me to bring Mette with me?' Aksel wondered if a child might be too much for Andy but he smiled.

'I'd like that. As long as she doesn't find me boring.' Andy glanced down at his leg. Aksel shook his head, sure that if anyone could see past Andy's injuries then his daughter could.

Flora broke in briskly. 'If you send me the pictures, I can print them out for you. Perhaps Mette will be able to see them better that way?'

'Thanks. I think she will.'

The two men nodded goodbye, and Flora followed as Andy walked slowly towards the doorway. She turned, giving Aksel a grin.

'If you're at a loose end, you can always go and sculpt something else. I'm very partial to unicorns, and now you have this down to a fine art it should be child's play...'

'Don't listen to her, man.' Andy called out the words. 'She's far too bossy.'

Bossy and beautiful. Soft and sweet and yet surprisingly strong. Intelligent, warm... The list just went on. Aksel had given up trying to complete it, because there was always more to say about Flora.

He called out an acknowledgement to Andy, wondering if Flora had lip-read the words that had formed silently on his lips. Or maybe she'd tapped into the connection between them and she just knew, because she shot him a look of amused surprise.

You want a unicorn...? If that was what Flora wanted, then that's what she'd get.

The ice unicorn stood next to the reindeer, and Ted Mackie had told Aksel that it had attracted both attention and admiration. He hadn't told Flora about it, even though she was the one person that it was intended to please. She was sure enough to hear about it, and he hoped she'd know it was *her* unicorn.

He'd arranged a schedule with Lyle for

when he should bring Mette home. Both of them agreed that Mette was settling in well, and Aksel was anxious that she wouldn't miss any of the activities that the clinic ran for its patients.

'Are you sure you're happy with this? It's a little less than we originally envisaged.' Lyle gave him a searching look, and Aksel realised that his own attitude had changed since they'd last spoken about this. The question was less of a tug of war and more a meeting of minds now.

'I'm very happy with it. My relationship with Mette has been much better since she's been here. I have you to thank for that. She's gained a lot of confidence.' Aksel had wondered if he should say that Flora had given *him* the confidence to see that.

Lyle had nodded, smiling. 'I'm glad you feel that way. I think that your daily visits are very important for Mette, she knows that you're always there for her.'

He'd gone to the children's unit to see Mette and she'd greeted him with a hug and a kiss. When he'd asked her if she'd like to spend the day with him tomorrow, she'd tugged at the play assistant's arm excitedly, telling her that she was going to explore a new place with her papa.

Then he'd texted Flora, asking her if she was free. There had been no mention of unicorns, which had been a little disappointing, but her 'Yes' had made up for that.

Aksel arrived at the clinic just as the children were finishing their breakfast. He packed some things into his day-pack, although in truth nothing was needed. But Mette liked the idea of packing for a journey.

His shoulder had improved a great deal. The massage had done wonders and he suspected that Flora's wake-up call had something to do with it as well. He lifted Mette up onto his shoulders, perched on top of his day-pack, and felt his stride lengthen as they started the two-mile walk home, the rhythm of his steps quieting his heart. Aksel began to tell Mette the story of his trip up to a remote village in the Andes.

'Were there crocodiles, Papa?'

Not that he'd noticed. But, then, Mette's idea of a crocodile was her smiling stuffed toy. 'Yes, there were crocodiles. We gave them some chocolate so they wouldn't eat us.'

'And penguins?'

'Yes. We had to go fishing and catch them some tea, so they'd tell us the right way to the village.' If he was going to enter into the realms of fantasy, then he may as well just go for it.

'Did your feet hurt?'

'A little bit. I had a big blister on my toe.' He'd made a rookie mistake on the way back down, allowing water to get inside one of his boots, and frostbite had taken hold.

'Did it get better, Papa?'

'Yes, it got better. And when we reached the village, at the top of the high snowy mountain, the people there welcomed us and gave us food and comfortable beds, with warm quilts like yours.'

Mette whooped with joy, and the achievement seemed greater than the walk up to the isolated village, in terrible weather conditions, had been.

They had warm drinks together when they arrived back at the cottage, and Mette insisted on keeping her hat on, since she too was an explorer. Then there was a knock at the door, and

Flora burst into the cottage, bringing the same sunlight with her that she took everywhere.

'I like the new look.' She grinned up at him and Aksel's hand shot awkwardly to the small plait that ran from his right temple and was caught into the elastic band that held the rest of his hair back.

'Mette's rag doll has plaits...' He shrugged as if it was nothing. When Mette had demanded that she be allowed to plait his hair this morning, it had felt like another step towards intimacy with his daughter, and he hadn't had the heart to unravel the uneven braid.

'I'm glad you kept it. She has excellent taste.' Flora obviously approved wholeheartedly. 'I hear that Ted Mackie's acquired an ice unicorn...'

Aksel wondered if she really hadn't been to see it, or she was just teasing. 'Has he?' He decided to play things cool.

'It's beautiful. I have about a million pictures of it.' She stood on her toes, kissing his cheek so briefly that he only realised she'd done it after the fact. 'Thank you.'

His cheek tingled from the touch of her lips as he followed Flora into the sitting room, where Mette was playing with Kari. Aksel decided that the hours spent sculpting the unicorn had been well worth it, and that he'd be tempted to create a whole menagerie of fantastic creatures in exchange for one more fleeting kiss.

It was agreed that they would walk down to the marketplace to see the village Christmas tree and the Christmas market. Aksel called Kari, putting on the yellow vest that denoted that she was at work now.

'Mette's already using Kari as her assistance dog?'

'No, but Esme suggested that it might be a good idea to let her see her at work a bit, just to get her used to the idea. Where's Dougal?'

'I took him up to the therapy centre, they're minding him. I didn't want him to get under Mette's feet.' Flora took a green and red striped bobble hat from the pocket of her red coat, pulling it down over her ears, and Aksel chuckled. She looked delightful.

'What are you? One of Santa's elves?'

'Right in one.' She shot him an innocent look, tugging at the hat. 'What gave me away?'

CHAPTER TEN

CLUCHLOCHRY'S MARKET SQUARE was paved with cobblestones, and boasted an old market cross, worn and battered by many winters. The market was already in full swing, with fairy lights hung around the canvas-topped stalls, and the village Christmas tree standing proudly in one corner, smothered in lights. As this was a Saturday morning, carol singers and a band had turned out to give the market a festive air.

The band struck up a melody that Mette recognised, and she started to sing along in Norwegian. Aksel lifted her up out of the crush of people, and heard Flora singing too, in English. At the end of the carol she joined in with the round of applause for the band, and Mette flung her arms up, wriggling with delight.

'Shall we go over to the village hall first?' Flora indicated a stone building next to the church. 'There are lots of stalls in there as well.'

Aksel nodded his agreement, and Flora led the way, while he followed with Mette. Kari trotted by her side, and every now and then the little girl held out her hand, putting it on Kari's back. It was a start. Soon, hopefully, Mette would be learning to rely on Kari to guide her.

Inside, it looked as if there had been some kind of competition between the stallholders to see who could get the most Christmas decorations into their allotted space. Aksel saw a large reindeer twinkling above one of them, and decided not to point it out to Mette, in case she wanted to take it home with her.

'Oh, look.' Flora had caught sight of yet another stall that she wanted to visit. 'I heard that Aileen was here, we should go and see her knitwear. She might have something that Mette would like.'

Aksel nodded his agreement, and Flora led him over to the stall, introducing him to Aileen Sinclair, an older woman with greying hair, confiding the information that Aileen was Lyle's mother and that she did a *lot* of knitting. That was self-evident from the racks of hats and scarves, and the sweaters laid out on two tables. Aileen smiled at him, sizing him up with an experienced eye.

'I don't know whether I can find anything to fit you, hen.' Aileen seemed willing to try all the same, sorting through a small pile of chunky cableknit sweaters. 'No, there isn't much call for extra-large, and Mrs Bell bought the last one for her son. If there's something you like, we can always make it up for you.'

'Thank you.' Aksel began to dutifully look through the sweaters. 'Actually, we were looking for something for my daughter.'

Flora lifted Mette up so that she could run her hand across the fine, lace knitted children's jumpers. Aileen greeted Mette with another of her beaming smiles, producing a tape measure from her pocket, and began to measure Mette's arms.

'What colour do you like, Mette?' Flora always asked Mette what she liked rather than suggesting things to her.

'Red.' Mette had caught sight of Aileen's bright red sweater, under her coat.

'Very good choice. Maybe a lacy one?' Aileen glanced at Flora and she nodded.

Piles of sweaters were looked through, knocked over and then re-stacked, in what looked like a completely arbitrary search. Finally three pretty sweaters, which looked to be around Mette's size, were laid out on top of the others.

'What do you think, Aksel?' Flora turned to him questioningly.

'They're all very nice.' Aksel wasn't prepared to commit himself any further than that and Flora frowned at him.

'You're no help.'

'Everyone should stick to what they're good at.' And Flora was very good at shopping. She always seemed to pick out the nicest things, buying the best she could afford and yet not over-spending. That was why she always looked immaculate.

He watched as Flora encouraged Mette to run her hand across each of the sweaters to feel their softness and warmth. She picked one, and Flora unzipped her coat so that Aileen could hold it up against her and make sure it fitted properly. The general consensus of opinion seemed to be that this was the perfect sweater, and Aksel reached into his pocket for his wallet.

He was too slow. As Aileen wrapped the sweater carefully in pretty paper, sticky-taping the ends down, Flora had whipped a note from her purse and handed it over.

'Thank you. I'll get your change.' Aileen plumped the package into a paper carrier bag and gave it to Mette.

'Don't worry about the change, Aileen. You don't charge enough for these already, I still have the one I bought from you three years ago. You'd make a lot more money if you didn't make them to last.'

Aileen flushed with pleasure. The sweaters were clearly more a labour of love than a money-making exercise.

Mette whirled around, eager to show Aksel her carrier bag, and Flora caught her before she lost her balance. He examined the bag, declared it wonderful, and Aileen bade them a cheery goodbye.

Then it was on to the other stalls. Flora was endlessly patient, letting Mette sniff each one of the home-made soaps on offer and choose the one she liked the best. The avuncular man at the fudge stall offered them some samples to taste, and Aksel was allowed to make the choice of which to buy. The indoor market was a whirl of colours, tastes, textures and smells, and Aksel found himself enjoying it as much as Mette obviously was.

'Are you hungry yet?' Flora clearly was or she wouldn't have asked the question. 'There's a pub on the other side of the green that serves family lunches whenever the market's open.'

A family lunch. That sounded good, and not just because Aksel was hungry too. He could really get used to this feeling of belonging, with both Mette *and* Flora.

'Good idea. They won't mind us taking Kari in?' Despite her yellow service coat, Kari wasn't working as Mette's assistance dog just yet.

'No, of course not. They're used to people coming in with dogs from the canine therapy centre, and they welcome them.'

Flora managed to find a table close to one of the roaring fires, and while she stripped off Mette's coat, Aksel went to the bar, ordering thick vegetable soup with crusty bread, and two glasses of Christmas punch. When he returned with the tray, Mette and Flora were investigating their purchases together. This seemed to be an integral part of the shopping experience, and Mette was copying Flora, inserting her finger into the corner of each package so that they could catch a glimpse of what was inside.

'Why don't you open them?' Aksel began to clear a space on the table between them, and Flora shot him a horrified look.

'Hush! We can't open them until we get home.'

'Ah. All right.' Aksel found that the thought of Flora and Mette spreading out their purchases for a second and more thorough inspection was just as enticing as this was. This complex ritual was more than just going out and shopping for something that met your needs. It was about bonding and sharing, and the excitement of finding a sweater that was the right colour and design, and fitted perfectly.

He was learning that there were many things he *could* share with Mette, and wondered if this would ever be one of them. At the moment, it seemed an impossible set of rules and conventions, which were as complicated as any he'd seen on his travels. It occurred to him that

Mette really needed a mother, and the thought wasn't as difficult to come to terms with as it had been. He could be a good father, without having to do everything himself.

Flora and Mette were whispering together, and he couldn't hear what they were saying over the swell of conversation around them. Then Flora turned to him, her eyes shining.

'We're giving you ten out of ten. Possibly ten and a half.'

That sounded great, but he wasn't sure what he'd done to deserve it. 'What for?'

'For being our ideal shopping companion.' Flora didn't seem disposed to break the score down, but Mette had no such reservations.

'Because you carry the bags, Papa. And you don't rush, and you buy soup. And fudge.'

Aksel hadn't realised that this could cause him so much pride. And pleasure. 'Thank you. I'm…honoured.'

Mette gave him a nod, which said that he was quite right to feel that way, having been given such an accolade. Flora smiled, and suddenly his whole world became warm and full of sparkle.

'The Christmas tableau will be open by the

time we've finished. And then I'd like to pop over to Mary's stall if you don't mind. I heard she has some nice little things for Christmas gifts.'

'That sounds great. I'd like that.' He wasn't quite sure what a Christmas tableau was, but he'd go with the flow. Aksel leaned back in his seat, stretching his legs out towards the fire. Making sense of the proceedings didn't much matter, he'd been voted ten out of ten as a shopping companion, and that was a great deal more than good enough.

The Christmas tableau turned out to be housed in a three-sided wooden structure outside the church. Inside were Mary and Joseph, an assortment of shepherds and three kings, along with one of the dogs from the therapy centre. Aksel wasn't quite sure how it had ended up there, but he assumed its presence had something to do with Esme, and that she'd probably had a hand in choosing its festive, red and white dog coat.

'Mette!' As they opened the gate to the churchyard, the shortest and broadest of the three kings started to wave, handing a jewelled box to one of the other kings and ducking past the crowd that was forming around the tableau.

Mette turned her head, recognising the voice, and tugged at Aksel's hand. 'It's Carrie. Where is she?'

It was the first time that Aksel had heard Mette say anything like that. Usually she ignored the things she couldn't see, and she'd been known to throw a temper tantrum when she couldn't find something she wanted.

'She's coming over to you now, sweetheart.' Flora volunteered the information, and Mette nodded. Now that the king was a little closer, he realised it *was* Carrie, one of the children's nurses from the clinic, and almost unrecognisable under a false beard and a large jewelled hat. Her small frame was completely disguised by what looked like several layers of bulky clothes under her costume.

'Hi, Carrie. Keeping warm?' Flora grinned at her.

'I'm a bit hot, actually.' Carrie pushed her beard up, propping it incongruously on the rim of her hat, and bent down to greet Mette. 'The costume was a bit big so I've got two coats on underneath this. Along with a thick sweater *and* thermal underwear.'

'Sounds reasonable to me. You've got a couple of hours out here. The shepherds are already looking a bit chilly.'

'Don't worry about them. The vicar's brought a couple of Thermos flasks along, and we've got an outdoor heater behind the manger, that's why everyone's crowding around it. You'd be surprised how warm it gets after a while.' Carrie volunteered the information and Flora laughed.

'That's good to know. I'll make sure I'm standing next to the heater when it's my turn.'

It was impossible that Flora wouldn't take a turn, she was so much a part of the life of the village. Aksel wondered what she'd be dressing up as and decided to wait and see.

'Would you like to come and see the stable, Mette?' Carrie bent down towards her. 'We've got a rabbit…'

'Yes, please.' Mette took her hand, waving to Aksel as Carrie led her away.

'A rabbit?' Aksel murmured the words as he watched her go.

'The vicar's not afraid to improvise, and I

don't think there were any sheep available.'
Flora chuckled. 'And anyway, don't you think
it's the best stable you've ever seen?'

It was. The costumes were great, and there
was a sturdy manger and lots of straw. A couple of other children, besides Mette, had been
led up to the tableau by their parents, and had
been welcomed inside by the shepherds and
kings. Carrie was carefully showing Mette
around, talking to her and allowing her to
touch everything. The place shone with sparkling lights to re-create stars, and the warmth
and love of a small community.

'Yes. The very best.'

CHAPTER ELEVEN

AKSEL WAS RELAXED and smiling as they watched Mette explore the stable with Carrie. So different from the man Flora had first met. The clinic tended to do that to patients and their families. Flora had seen so many people arrive looking tense and afraid, and had watched the secure and welcoming environment soothe their fears and allow them to begin to move forward. It was always good to see, but she'd never been so happy about it as she was now.

It was hard not to wonder what things might have been like if she and Aksel had met before they'd both been changed by the world. Whether they might have been able to make a family for more than just the space of a day. But for all the hope that the clinic brought to people's hearts, there was also the understanding that some things couldn't be changed, and it was necessary to make the best of them.

She should enjoy today for what it was, and let it go.

Carrie delivered Mette back to her father, and she chattered brightly about having seen the rabbit and stroked it, as they walked towards Mary's stall. It was a riot of colour. Along with a few small quilts, there were fabric bags, with appliquéd flowers, patchwork lavender bags tied with ribbon, and quilted hats with earflaps. Mary was, unusually, not in the thick of things but sitting on a rickety stool and leaving her husband and Jackie, the young mum who helped out in the shop on Saturdays, to deal with the customers.

Flora greeted her with a smile. 'Hello, Mary. It's cold enough out here…'

Mary was sitting with her hands in her pockets, and her woollen hat pulled down over her ears and brow. Most of the stallholders prided themselves on being out in all weather, however cold, but maybe Mary should consider going into the pub for a while to get warm.

Mary nodded, her expression one of deep thought.

'These look wonderful.' Flora indicated the

lavender bags and Aksel hoisted Mette up so she could smell them. 'How much are they?'

Mary smiled suddenly. 'Thruppence.'

Okay…. Flora had never heard of thruppenny lavender bags being a thing, but there were three in each bundle. They'd be tagged with a price anyway. Mary went back to staring in her husband's direction and Flora wondered if maybe they'd had an argument about something.

Hats were tried on, lavender sniffed, and the fabric bags admired. They found a hat for Mette, its bright reds and greens matching her coat, and Aksel encouraged Flora to treat herself to one of the fabric bags. It would be perfect for carrying some of the smaller items that she used most regularly in the course of her job, and it would be nice to visit the residents at the sheltered living complex carrying a bag that didn't scream that it was *medical.*

Mary smiled at her, and Flora put the bag and the hat down in front of her. 'I'd like to take these, Mary.'

'Ah, yes.' Mary sprang to her feet. 'The hat's for…the little girl.'

It was unlike Mary to forget a name. 'Yes, it's for Mette.'

'Of course. Red.' Mary stared at the hat and then seemed to come to her senses. 'That's two pounds for the hat, plus three and fourpence for the bag. Fourteen and six altogether, dear.'

Mary held out her hand to receive the money. Something was very wrong. Flora leaned across, studying her face in the reflection of the fairy lights above their heads.

'Are you all right, Mary?'

'I just have a bit of a headache, dear. How much did I say it was?'

Mary *wasn't* all right. Flora glanced at Aksel and saw concern on his face too. Even if he didn't follow the vagaries of pounds, shillings and pence, it was obvious that Mary was confused and calculating the bill in coins that had been obsolete for almost fifty years.

Flora squeezed around the edge of the stall, taking Mary's hand. It felt ice-cold in hers. 'Mary, can you sit down for me, please?'

'No, dear.'

'What's the matter?' Mary's husband, John, had left the customer he was serving and come over to see what was happening.

'I don't know. Mary doesn't seem well, has she hit her head or anything recently?'

John Monroe had been a county court judge before he'd retired, and his avuncular manner covered an ability to sum up a situation quickly and take action.

'Sit down, hen.' He guided Mary to the stool, keeping his arm around her when she sank down onto it, and turning to Flora. 'She bumped her head when we were setting up the stall. She said it was nothing, and she seemed fine...'

'Okay, where?' Flora gently peeled off Mary's hat and realised she hadn't needed to ask. A large bump was forming on the side of her head.

'We need to get her into the warm, John.' Flora looked around at the crowded market. 'Go and fetch the vicar. I think that the church is the best place.'

John hesitated, not wanting to leave Mary, and Flora caught his arm. 'Go now, please.'

Aksel had dropped their shopping bags and Jackie stowed them away under the stall. Mette seemed to understand that something was wrong, and she stood quietly, her arms around Kari's neck. Jackie took her hand and Aksel bent down next to Mary, supporting her on the stool. Flora pulled out her phone.

'I'm going to call Charles.' She hoped that she wasn't overreacting but in her heart she knew that she wasn't. And she knew that Charles Ross-Wylde would rather she called, if she thought someone needed his help.

Charles answered on the second ring, and Flora quickly told him what had happened, answering his questions and breathing a sigh of relief when he told her he'd be there as soon as he could. She ended the call, and Aksel glanced up at her.

'Charles is on his way, and he's going to call an ambulance.' Flora murmured the words quietly, so that Mary didn't hear. 'This may be a bad concussion or a brain bleed, so we must be very careful with her and take her somewhere warm and quiet.'

'Fourteen and six… Fourteen…and…seven…' Mary seemed to be in a world of her own, and Aksel nodded, concern flashing in his eyes.

The vicar arrived, along with Carrie, who was red-faced and breathless from running, her beard hanging from one ear. She took Mette's hand and Aksel turned to her.

'Will you take her, please, Carrie?'

'Of course. You see to Mary, and I'll look after Mette and Kari.'

'I'll go and open up the church lounge.' The vicar was fumbling under his shepherd's costume for his keys. 'It's nice and warm in there.'

Now all they had to do was to persuade Mary to go with them. Flora knelt down beside her. 'Mary, we're going to the church.'

'Are we?' Mary gazed dreamily around her, as if she wasn't quite sure what direction that was. 'All right.'

Mary went to stand up, swaying suddenly as she lost her balance. Aksel caught her, lifting her up, and she lay still and compliant in his arms.

People were gathering around the stall, some offering help. The only help they could give was to stand back, and Flora cleared a path for Aksel. As everyone began to realise what was happening, the crowd melted away in front of them, leaving them a clear route to the church.

They walked around the side of the ancient building to a more modern annexe. The vicar was waiting for them, holding the swing doors open, and he ushered Aksel through to the quiet, comfortable lounge. There was a long, upholstered bench seat at one side of the room, and Aksel carefully laid Mary down, while Flora fetched a cushion for her head.

'Mary, love....' John knelt down beside her and took her hand, but Mary snatched it away. Aksel laid his hand on John's shoulder.

'She's confused, John. We just need to keep her calm at the moment.'

'Is there any tea?' Mary tried to sit up, and Aksel gently guided her back down again.

'The vicar's just making some. He'll be along in a minute.' His answer seemed to satisfy Mary, and she lay back. Aksel kept talking to her, reassuring her and keeping her quiet.

Flora's phone rang and she pulled it from her pocket. Charles sounded as if he was in the car, and she quickly told him where to find them.

'That's great. I'll be there soon, and an ambulance is on its way too...' The call fizzled and cut out, and Flora put her phone back into her pocket. Maybe Charles had just driven into a black spot, or maybe he'd said all he wanted to say.

'What's the matter with her, Flora?' John was standing beside her, waiting for her to end the call.

'I'm not sure, but it seems to be a result of the bump on her head.' Flora didn't want to distress John even further by listing the things it could be. 'We need to keep her quiet. Charles is on his way and the ambulance will be here soon.'

'What have I done...?' Tears misted John's eyes. 'She said it was nothing. She seemed a bit subdued, but I thought she was just cold. I was going to take her to the pub for lunch as soon as I'd finished with the customer I was serving.'

'It's okay. In these situations people often try to deny there's anything wrong with them and they'll hide their symptoms. And they'll push away the people they love most. We'll get her to the hospital and they'll help her.' There was nothing more that Flora could say. If this was what she thought it was, then Mary was gravely ill.

John nodded. 'Is there *anything* I can do?'

'Has Mary taken any medication? Did she take something for the headache?'

'She didn't say she had one. And, no, she tries to avoid taking painkillers if she can.'

That could be a blessing in this particular situation. 'No aspirin, or anything like that? Please try to be sure.'

'No. Nothing. I've been with her all day, she hasn't taken anything.' John shook his head.

'Okay, that's good.' Flora smiled encouragingly at him. 'Now, I want you to sit down and write down exactly when Mary bumped her head, and how she's seemed since. Please include everything, whether you think it's important or not.'

'Right you are.'

Maybe John knew that Flora was giving him something to do but he tore a blank sheet from one of the stack of parish magazines that lay on top of the piano and hurried over to a chair, taking a pen from his jacket pocket. Maybe the details would come in useful...

Flora knelt down beside Aksel. 'You should go and get Mette now. I can manage.'

Flora didn't want him to leave. Her own medical knowledge was enough to care for Mary until Charles arrived, but he was so calm. So reassuringly capable. But however much Mary might need him, however much Flora *did* need him, she knew that he couldn't leave Mette.

'One minute…' He got to his feet, striding towards the door. A brief, quiet conversation with someone outside, and he returned.

'You're sure you want to stay?' Aksel had obviously made a decision and from the look on his face it troubled him a little. But he'd come back.

'Carrie's going to take Mette and Kari back to the clinic and I'll meet her there later. She's in very good hands.'

'Yes, she is. Thank you.'

He gave a little nod, and knelt back down beside Mary, taking her hand. Flora had to think now. She had to remember all the advanced first-aid courses she'd been on, and the physiology and pathology elements of her degree course. She took a deep breath.

Leaning forward, she looked for any blood or fluid discharge from Mary's ears and nose. Checked that she was conscious and alert, and noticed that her pupils were of an unequal size and that a bruise was forming behind her ear. Then she picked up Mary's hand.

'Can you squeeze my hand, Mary?'

The pressure from Mary's fingers was barely noticeable.

'As tight as you can.'

'I think I must have hurt it.' Mary looked up at her, unthinking, blank trust written on her face. It tore at Flora's heart, and she knew that she must do everything she could to help Mary.

'Let me massage it for you.' It wouldn't do her head injury any good, but it would keep Mary calm, and that was important.

'Thank you. I feel a bit sick.'

Aksel carefully moved Mary, sitting her up, and Flora grabbed the rubbish bin, emptying it out on the floor. Mary retched weakly, and then relaxed.

'That's better. I'm sorry...'

'It's okay. You're okay now.' Flora made sure that Mary's mouth was clear, and Aksel gently laid her down in the recovery position. Flora was aware that John was watching them, and couldn't imagine his agony, but she had to concentrate on Mary.

She talked to Mary, soothing her, watching her every reaction. It seemed a very long time before the door opened and the vicar ushered Charles into the room.

John shot to his feet, watching and listening. Flora carefully relayed all the information she had to Charles, and he nodded, bending down towards Mary to examine her. Mary began to fret again, and by the time he'd finished she was trying to push him away. Charles beckoned to Flora.

'Can you keep her quiet?'

'Yes.' Flora knelt down, taking Mary's hand, and she seemed to settle. She heard Charles talking softly to John behind her, and then the arrival of the ambulance crew. Then she had to move back as the paramedics lifted Mary carefully onto a stretcher.

'I couldn't have done better myself, Flora. Well done.' Charles didn't wait for her answer, turning to usher John out of the room.

The lights from the ambulance outshone the fairy lights on the stalls in the marketplace. The noise and bustle seemed to have quietened down, and many of the stallholders watched as Mary was lifted into the ambulance and Charles and John followed.

Suddenly she felt Aksel's arm around her shoulders. As the ambulance negotiated the narrow street around the perimeter of the market square, people began to crowd around her, wanting to know what had happened to Mary.

'I'm sorry, we can't say exactly what's happened, that's for the doctors at the hospital to decide. Mary's in good hands.' Aksel gave the answer that Flora was shaking too much to give. Then he hurried her over to Mary's stall.

'Jackie, will you be okay to pack up the stall?'

Jackie nodded. 'Yes, I've called my husband and he's on his way down with his mates. They'll be here in a minute. How's Mary?'

'I'm afraid we don't know, but Charles Ross-Wylde is with her and she's in very good hands.' Aksel repeated the very limited reassurance that he'd given to everyone else.

'Okay. I'll wait for news. Carrie came and took your shopping bags, she's taken them back to the clinic with Mette.'

'Thanks, Jackie. Are you sure you'll be all right on your own?'

'Yes, of course. Look, there's my husband now.'

Jackie waved, and Aksel nodded. He turned away, his arm tightly around Flora.

'Do you want to go the long way home? Or take the more direct route?'

'What's the long way? Via Istanbul?'

Aksel chuckled. 'No, via the clinic. I'm going to go home and pick up the SUV, then go to see Mette. I'll either walk you home or you can come with me.'

'I'll come with you.' Being at home alone didn't much appeal at the moment. 'Thanks for staying with me, Aksel. I know you didn't want to leave Mette.'

'No, I didn't. But Mette was all right and I reckoned I might be needed here.'

'Yes, you were.' Flora was going through all of the things she'd done in her head, trying to think of something that she'd missed. Something she might have done better.

'Mary's going to be all right. Largely because of you...'

'You're just saying that. I'm not a doctor.'

'No, but you used your medical knowledge to do as much as any doctor on the scene could have. You kept her quiet, you made sure she didn't choke. You acted professionally and decisively.'

'But if something happens to her...' Flora

didn't want to think about it. If there was something that she'd missed, and Mary didn't survive this… She couldn't bear to think about it.

He stopped walking, turning to face her. His eyes seemed dark, and his shadow all-encompassing.

'Listen. Mary was surrounded by people, and no one realised there was something wrong. If you hadn't noticed and done something about it, this wouldn't have ended as well as it has. You were the one who gave her a chance, Flora.'

His trust in her reached the dark corners of her heart. 'You were pretty cool-headed yourself.'

'Well, I've been in a few situations before.'

Flora would bet he had. 'I don't know what I would have done without you.'

He chuckled. 'I do. You would have done exactly the same—taken care of Mary, checked all her symptoms, and acted quickly. I might not cross the line from animal medicine into human medicine, but those things are essential in any kind of emergency.'

'You make me feel so much better.' He'd

lifted a heavy weight from her shoulders. Whatever happened now, she'd know that she'd done all she could.

'Mary was lucky that you were there, Flora. Never think otherwise.'

They'd reached the SUV, parked outside his cottage, and Aksel felt in his pocket for the keys and opened the door for Flora. He was clearly keen to see Mette. *She* wanted to see Mette. Both of them had found a place in her heart, and now she didn't want to let them go.

The process of winding down had taken a while, but helping Mette to unpack the bags that lay in the corner of the room had helped. Aksel had been persuaded to tell a story about his travels, and she found herself joining in with Mette's excitement at the twists and turns of his narrative.

As they were leaving her phone rang. She pulled it out of her pocket, seeing Charles's number on the display, and when she answered, she heard John's voice on the line.

She listened carefully to what he had to say, feeling the tension ebb out of her. 'That's really good news, John...'

'Words can't express my gratitude, for what you did this afternoon Flora...' John's voice was breaking with emotion.

'I'm glad I could help. Make sure you get some rest tonight, you'll be able to see her in the morning. I'll come as soon as she's allowed visitors.' Flora ended the call, aware suddenly that Aksel was staring at her, waiting to hear John's news.

'This isn't bad news, is it?'

Flora shook her head. 'No, it's very good news. We were right about it being a brain haemorrhage and Mary was taken into surgery straight away. The operation was a success, and they're hopeful that, in time, Mary will make a full recovery.'

'That's wonderful. How's John, does he need a lift from the hospital? I can go there now and take him home.'

'No, he's okay. Charles is still there and he got someone from the estate to fetch his car from the village and bring it to the hospital. Benefits of being the Laird.' A great weight seemed to have been lifted from Flora's chest, and she felt that she could really breathe again. 'John said...he was glad that I'd been there.'

'Yes. I was glad you were there, too. Let's go home, shall we?'

It seemed so natural to just nod and take his arm. As if the home that they were going to was *their* home and not two separate cottages. As they walked out of the clinic together, towards the battered SUV, it didn't seem to matter that she was leaning on his arm. Just for tonight, until she reached her own front door, she could rely on Aksel's strength and support.

CHAPTER TWELVE

FLORA HAD BEEN wondering whether to ask Aksel over for Sunday lunch, but she'd seen him set out towards the clinic with Kari by his side at eleven o'clock. She opened the refrigerator, staring at its contents. Suddenly she didn't feel like going to the trouble of cooking.

She made herself a sandwich, rounding it off with apple pie and ice cream as she watched a film on TV. Then she picked up a book, curling up on the sofa with Dougal and working her way through a couple of chapters.

The doorbell rang, and she opened her front door to find Aksel standing in the front porch. 'Shouldn't you be at the clinic?' The question slipped out before she'd had time to think.

'I went in a little early today and had lunch with Mette. I left her making paper angels with the other children.'

There was always something going on at the

clinic, and Mette had obviously been drawn into the Sunday afternoon activities. 'That's good. The world always needs more paper angels.'

He nodded. 'Would you like to come for a walk?'

'A walk? I was planning to sit by the fire and make a few welcome gifts for the kids.'

'Sounds nice. A lot less chilly.' Something in his eyes beckoned her.

'The forecast's for snow later on this evening.'

He nodded, looking up at the sky. 'That looks about right. Are you coming?'

It was a challenge. Aksel was asking her to trust him, and in Flora's experience trusting a man didn't usually end well.

But Aksel was different. And what could happen on a windy, snowy hillside? Certainly nothing that involved exposing even a square inch of flesh.

'Why not? Come in, I'll get my coat.'

'You'll need a pair of sturdy shoes.' He glanced at the shoe rack in the hall.

'Even *I* wouldn't tackle the countryside in high heels. I have walking boots.' They were right at the back of the wardrobe, and Flora made for the stairs.

When she came back downstairs, his gaze flipped from her boots to the thick water-proof coat she wore and he gave a little nod of approval. As he strode across the road and towards the woods ahead of them, Flora struggled to keep up and he slowed a little.

'Where are we going?'

'I thought up to the old keep.' He pointed to the hilltop that overlooked the village, where piles of stones and a few remnants of wall were all that was left of the original castle seat of the Ross-Wylde family. 'Is that too far?'

It looked a long way. The most direct route from the village was up a steep incline, and Aksel was clearly heading for the gentler slope at the other side, which meant they had to go through the woods first.

'I can make it.' She wasn't going to admit to any doubts. 'Looks like a nice route for a Sunday afternoon.'

He kept his face impressively straight. If Aksel had any doubts about her stamina, he'd obviously decided to set them aside in response to her bravado. Perhaps he reckoned that he could always carry her for part of the way.

'I think so.' His stride lengthened again, as if he'd calculated the exact speed they'd need to go to get back by teatime. Flora fell into step with him, finding that the faster pace wasn't as punishing as it seemed, and they walked together along the path that led into the trees.

The light slowly began to fail. Flora hoped they'd be home soon, although Aksel didn't seem averse to stumbling around in the countryside after dark. She felt her heel begin to rub inside her boot and wondered if she hadn't bitten off more than she could chew.

Only their footsteps sounded in the path through the trees. It was oddly calming to walk beside him in silence, both travelling in the same direction without any need for words. Their heads both turned together as the screaming bark of a fox came from off to their left, and in the gathering gloom beneath the trees Flora began to hear the rustle of small creatures, which she generally didn't stop to notice.

He stopped at the far end of the wood, and Flora was grateful for the chance to catch her breath. Aksel was staring ahead of him at a red-gold sunset flaming across the horizon. It was nothing new, she'd seen sunsets before. But stumbling upon this one seemed different.

'You're limping. Sit down.' He indicated a tree trunk.

Flora had thought she was making a pretty good job of *not* limping. 'I'm okay.'

'First rule of walking. Look after your feet. Sit.' He was brooking no argument and Flora plumped herself down on the makeshift seat. Aksel knelt in front of her, picking up her foot, and testing the boot to see if it would shift.

'Ow! Of course it's going to hurt if you do that…' she protested, and he ignored her, unlacing the boot. He stripped off her thin sock, the cold air making her toes curl.

'You're getting a blister.' He balanced her foot on his knee, reaching into his pocket and pulling out a blister plaster. It occurred to Flora that maybe he'd come prepared for her as she couldn't imagine that he ever suffered from blisters.

All the same, it was welcome. He stuck the plaster around her heel, and then pulled a pair of thick walking socks from his pocket.

'Your feet are moving around in your boots. These should help.'

'I thought walking boots were meant to be roomy.' She stared at the socks. They had *definitely* been brought along for her benefit.

'They're meant to fit. When your foot slips around in them, that's going to cause blisters.' He slid her boot back on and relaced it. 'How does that feel?'

She had to admit it. 'Better. Thanks.'

He nodded, unlacing her other boot. Running his fingers around her heel to satisfy himself that there were no blisters, he held the other sock out and she slid her foot into it. She reached for her boot, and he gave her a sudden smile.

'Let me do it. You need to lace them a bit tighter.'

Flora gave in to the inevitable. 'Rookie mistake?'

'Yes.' His habitual honesty wasn't making her feel any better.

'You might mention that it can happen to anyone. With new boots.' The boots weren't exactly new, but they hadn't been used much.

'It *can* happen to anyone. I let water get into

one of my boots once, and lost the tips of two toes to frostbite.'

'Hmm. Careless.'

He looked up at her, smiling suddenly. 'Yes, it was. Looking at the way your teammates are walking comes as second nature because your feet are the only things you have to carry you home.'

They weren't exactly in the middle of nowhere. One of the roads through the estate was over to their right, and Flora had her phone in her pocket, so she could always call a taxi. But as Aksel got to his feet, holding out his hand to help her up, that seemed about as impossible as if they'd been at the South Pole.

She took a couple of steps. 'That's much more comfortable.'

'Good. Let me know if they start to hurt again, I have more plasters.'

Of course he did. If there was a next time, she'd make him hand over the plasters and lace her boots herself. She'd show him that she could walk just as far as he could. Or at least to the top of the hill and back down again.

As the ground began to rise, Flora's determination was tested again. She put her head down, concentrating on just taking one step after another. The incline on the far side of the hill hadn't looked that punishing, but it was a different matter when you were walking up it.

Aksel stopped a few times, holding out his hand towards her, and she ignored him. She could do this herself. It was beginning to get really dark now, and snow started to sting her face. This was *not* a pleasant Sunday afternoon stroll.

Finally they made it to the top and Aksel stopped, looking around at the looming shapes of the stones. Flora would have let out a cheer if she'd had the breath to do it.

'Perhaps we should take a rest now. Before we go back down.'

Yes! It was cold up here, but there must be some place where the stones would shelter them. Flora's legs were shaking and she suddenly felt that she couldn't take another step. She followed him over to where a tree had grown up amongst the stones, its trunk almost a part of them, and sat down on a rock, worn smooth and flat from its exposed location. Heaven. Only heaven wasn't quite so cold.

'I won't be a minute. Stay there.'

She nodded. Wild horses couldn't get her to move now. Aksel strode away, the beam of his torch moving to and fro among the stones. He seemed to be looking for something. Flora bent over, putting her hands up to her ears to warm them.

When he returned he was carrying an armful of dry sticks and moss. Putting them down in front of her, he started to arrange them carefully in two piles.

'What are you going to do now? Rub two sticks together to make a fire?' Actually, a fire seemed like a very good idea. It was sheltered enough here from the snow, which was blowing almost horizontally now.

'I could do, if you want. But this is easier.' He produced a battered tin from his pocket, opening it and taking out a flint and steel. Expertly striking the flint along the length of the steel, a spark flashed, lighting the pile of tinder that he'd made. He carefully transferred the embers to the nest of branches, and flames sprang up.

This was *definitely* a good idea. Flora held her hands out towards the fire, feeling it begin to warm her face as Aksel fuelled it with some of the branches he'd set to one side. She felt herself beginning to smile, despite all he'd put her through.

'This is nice.' When he sat down next to her she gave him a smile.

'Better than your fire at home?' His tone suggested that he thought she'd probably say no.

'Yes. In a strange kind of way.' Flora was beginning to see how this appealed to Aksel. They'd only travelled a short way, but even though she could still see the lights of the village below her, she felt as if she was looking down from an entirely different planet. The effort of getting here had stripped everything away, and she felt unencumbered. Free, even.

CHAPTER THIRTEEN

AKSEL HAD PUSHED her hard, setting a pace that would stretch even an experienced walker. He'd wanted her exhausted, unable to sustain the smiles and the kindnesses that she hid behind and defended herself with. But Flora was a lot tougher than he'd calculated. She'd brushed away all his attempts to help her, and kept going until they'd got to the top of the hill.

But her smile *was* different now. As she warmed herself in front of the fire, Aksel could see her fatigue, and the quiet triumph in meeting the challenge and getting here. He'd found the real Flora, and he wasn't going to let her go if he could help it.

The blaze seemed to chase away the darkness that stood beyond it, illuminating the faces of the rocks piled around them as if this small shelter was the only place in the world. Right now, he wished it could be, because Flora was there with him.

'Now that we're here…' she flashed him a knowing smile '…what is it you want me to say?'

She knew exactly what he'd done. And it seemed that she didn't see the need for tact any more.

'Say whatever you want to say. What's said around a camp fire generally stays there.'

She thought for a moment. 'All right, then, since you probably have a lot more experience of camp-fire truth or dare games, you can start. What's the thing you most want?'

Tricky question. Aksel wanted a lot of things, but he concentrated on the one that he could wish for with a good conscience.

'Keeping Mette from harm.'

'That's a good one. You'll be needing to get some practice in before she hits her teens.'

'What's that supposed to mean?' Aksel explored the idea for a moment and then held up his hand to silence Flora. 'On second thoughts, I don't think I want to know.'

'That's just as well, really. Nothing prepares any of us for our teens.'

She was smiling, but there was quiet sadness in her tone. Aksel decided that if he didn't call her bluff now, he was never going to. This wasn't about Mette any more, it was all about Flora.

'All right. I'm going to turn the question on its head. What would you avoid if you could go back in time?'

'How long have you got?'

'There's plenty of fuel for the fire here. I'll listen for as long as I can convince you to stay.'

She stared into the fire, giving a little sigh. 'Okay. Number one is don't fret over spots. Number two is don't fall in love.'

'The spots I can do something about. I'm not sure that I'm the one to advise anyone about how not to fall in love.' Aksel was rapidly losing control of his own feelings for Flora.

'All you can do is be there for her when she finds herself with a broken heart.'

The thought was terrifying. But he wouldn't have to contend with Mette's teenage years just yet, and the question of Flora's heart was a more pressing one at the moment. He would never forgive himself if he lost this chance to ask.

'Who broke yours?'

'Mine?' Her voice broke a little over the word.

'Yes. What was his name?'

'Thomas Grant. I was nineteen. What was the name of the first girl who dumped you?'

Aksel thought hard. 'I don't remember. I went away on a summer camping trip with my friends, and by the time I got back she was with someone else. I don't think I broke her heart, and she didn't break mine.'

'If you can't remember her name, she probably didn't.' Flora was trying to keep this light, but these memories were obviously sad ones.'

'So… Thomas Grant. What did he do?'

'He…' Flora shrugged, as if it didn't matter. Aksel could tell that it did. He waited, hoping against agonised hope that if she looked into her own heart, and maybe his, she'd find some reason to go on.

'I went to university in Edinburgh to study physiotherapy. He was in the year above me, studying history…' She let out a sigh. 'I fell in love with him. I didn't tell my parents for a while, they were in Italy and I thought I'd introduce him to them first. I think my mum probably worked it out, though, and so Dad would have known as well.'

'An open secret, then.' It didn't sound so bad, but this had clearly hurt Flora. Aksel supposed that most really bad love affairs started well. The only real way to avoid hurt, was never to fall in love.

'Yes. We decided to tell our parents over the summer. We'd been talking about living together during our second year and…he seemed very serious. He even spoke about getting engaged. So I asked him to come to Italy with me for a fortnight. Mum and Dad really liked him and we had a great holiday. Alec wasn't too well that summer…'

Something prickled at the back of Aksel's neck. He knew that the end of this story wasn't a good one, and wondered what it could have to do with Flora's brother. His hand shook as he picked up a stick, poking the fire.

'You know, don't you, that cystic fibrosis is an inherited condition?' She turned to look at him suddenly.

'Yes.' Aksel searched his brain, locating the correct answer. 'It's a recessive gene, which means that both parents have to carry the gene

before there's any possibility of a child devel-
oping cystic fibrosis.'

'Yes, that's right. Tom knew that my brother
had cystic fibrosis, I never made any secret of
it and I'd explained that since both my parents
have the gene there was a good chance that I'd
inherited it from one of them. Not from both,
as my brother did, because I don't have the
condition.'

'There's also a chance you haven't.'

She nodded. 'There's a twenty five percent
chance of inheriting the gene from both parents. Fifty percent of inheriting it from one
parent, and a twenty five percent chance of
inheriting it from neither parent. The odds are
against me.'

She didn't know. The realisation thundered
through his head, like stampeding horses.
Aksel hadn't really thought about it, but taking the test to find out whether she'd inherited
the faulty gene seemed the logical thing to do,
and he wondered why Flora hadn't. He opened
his mouth and then closed it again, not sure
how to phrase the question.

'When we came home to Scotland, we went
to stay with his parents for a week. I told them

about myself, and talked about my family. Tom told me later that I shouldn't have said anything. His parents didn't want their grandchildren to run the risk of inheriting my genes.'

'But that's not something you have to keep a secret…' Aksel had tried to just let her tell the story, without intervening, but this was too much. Anger and outrage pulsed in his veins.

'No. I don't think so either.'

'But… Forgive me if this is the wrong thing to say, I'm sure your whole family would rather that your brother didn't have cystic fibrosis. That doesn't mean it would be better if your parents had never married, or your brother hadn't been born.'

Tears suddenly began to roll down her cheeks. Maybe he *had* said the wrong thing. 'Thank you. That's exactly how I feel.'

'So they were wrong.' Surely *someone* must have told her that. 'What did your parents say?'

'Nothing. I didn't tell them, or Alec. It would have really hurt them, and I couldn't tell my own brother that someone thought he wasn't good enough. He's a fine man, and he's found someone who loves him and wants to raise a family with him.'

The defiance in her voice almost tore his heart out. Flora had stayed silent in order to keep her brother from hurt. She'd borne it all by herself, and her tears told him that with no way to talk about it and work it through, the wound she'd been dealt had festered.

'Did he listen? To his parents?'

'Yes, he listened. It probably had a lot to do with the fact that they were funding his grant, and they threatened to withdraw their support if he didn't give me up.'

'Don't make excuses for him, Flora. Don't tell me that it's okay to even contemplate the thought that my daughter, or your brother, are worth less than anyone else.'

She laid her hand on his arm, and Aksel realised that he was shaking with rage. Maybe that was what she needed to see. Maybe this had hurt her for so long because she'd never talked about it, and never had the comfort of anyone else's reaction.

'No one's ever going to tell Mette that she's anything other than perfect. I'm not going to tell Alec that either.'

She'd missed herself out. Flora was perfect

too, whether or not she carried the gene. But, still, she hadn't found out…

'You don't know whether you carry the gene or not, do you?'

She shook her head miserably.

'Flora, it's no betrayal of your brother to want to know.'

'I know that. In my head.' She placed her hand over her heart. 'Not here…'

Suddenly it was all very clear to him. 'You just want someone to trust you, don't you?'

Surprise showed in her face. 'I never thought of it that way. But, yes, if I take the test I want someone who'll stick by me whatever the result. If it turns out that I don't carry the gene, then I'll never know what would have happened if I did, will I? I suppose that's just foolishness on my part.'

It was the foolishness of a woman who'd been badly hurt. One that Aksel could respect, and in that moment he found he could love it too, because it was Flora's.

'Anyone who really knew you would trust you, Flora. *I* trust you.'

She gave a little laugh. 'Are you making me an offer?'

Yes. He'd offer himself to her in a split second, no thought needed. But he couldn't gauge her mood, and the possibility that she might not be entirely serious made him cautious.

'I just meant that you can't allow this to stop you from taking what you want from life. You deserve a lot more than this.'

The sudden anger wasn't something that Flora usually felt. There was dull regret and the occasional throb of pain, but this was bright and alive. And it hurt, cutting into her like a newly sharpened blade.

'And that's why you brought me up here, is it? To take me apart, piece by piece?' On this hilltop, with the village laid out below them like a child's toy, it felt as if she could sense the world spinning. And it was spinning a great deal faster at the thought that Aksel wanted to know what made her tick.

'I brought you here because…it's possible to walk away from the everyday. To see things more clearly than you might otherwise. And because I wanted to know why someone as beautiful and accomplished as you are seems so sad.'

No. She couldn't hear this. Aksel needed to take the rose-coloured spectacles off and understand who she really was.

'I'm *not* sad. I just see things the way they are.'

'That no one's ever going to accept you for who you are? That's just not true, Flora.'

'Well that's not my experience. And for your information, I didn't give up on men completely, I just…approach with caution.'

He shook his head, giving a sudden snort of laughter. 'I've never thought that sex was much like stopping at a busy road junction.'

Trust Aksel. But his bluntness was always refreshing. She'd been skirting around the word and now that he'd said it… They were talking about sex. And unless Flora was very much mistaken, this wasn't a conversation about sex generally, it was about the two of them having sex. Despite all the reasons why it shouldn't, the thought warmed her.

'I'm not going to have sex with you, Aksel. I can't…' Flora didn't have the words to tell him why and she buried her face in her hands in frustration.'

'You don't have to give me any reasons. *No* is enough.'

Not many men took rejection the way that Aksel did. He'd pushed her on so many other things but this was where he drew the line. His smile let slip a trace of regret, but he accepted what she said as her final answer.

It wasn't final, though. Everything they were to each other, all the things they'd shared came crashing in on Flora. She couldn't let him believe that she didn't want him. The problem was hers, and she had to own it.

'It's not you. It's me.'

'It's a good decision, Flora. We've both been hurt. I'm leaving in five weeks, and you'll be staying here.'

And despite all that she wanted him. Maybe *because* of it. A relationship that had to end in five weeks didn't seem quite so challenging as something that might end because her genetic make-up, something she couldn't change, wasn't deemed good enough.

'But I *want* to explain...'

His face softened suddenly. 'There's no better place to do that than at a camp fire.'

'After Tom left me I had a few no-strings

affairs, with men I knew. I thought it would help me get over him, but…they just didn't turn out right.' Flora couldn't bring herself to be more specific than that. She was broken, and even Aksel couldn't mend her.

'They ended badly?' Aksel came to the wrong conclusion, which was hardly surprising. She was going to have to explain.

'No, they ended well, it was all very civilised. But things didn't work physically. For me, I mean…'

He was looking at her steadily. She could almost see his brain working, trying to fit each piece of the puzzle together, and when he did, she saw that too.

'I think that when two people have sex, an orgasm is something that you create together.'

Sex and *orgasm*. All in the same sentence and without a trace of embarrassment or hesitation. That made life a lot easier.

'I don't want to fake it with you, Aksel. And that's all I know how to do now.'

Tears began to roll down her cheeks. She wanted to be with him, and all that she'd lost hurt, in a way it never had before. Flora heard the scrape of Aksel's all-weather jacket as he reached for her, and she shied away.

'The way I see it is that we have a connection. I don't know why or how, but I do know that I want to be close to you, in whatever way seems right. Do you feel that?' The tenderness in his face made her want to cry even more.

'I feel it. But it's too late…' Flora made one last attempt to fight the growing warmth that wanted so much more than she was able to give.

'Maybe I just ask you to my place for a glass of wine. We put our feet up in front of the fire…'

Frustration made her open her mouth before she'd put her brain in gear. 'You don't get it, Aksel. I want wild and wonderful sex with you, and frankly a glass of wine doesn't even come close…' Flora clapped her hand over her mouth before she blurted anything else out.

The trace of a smile hovered around his lips. 'You're killing me, Flora. You know that, don't you?'

'I know. I'm sorry.'

'That's okay. You're worth every moment of it.' Aksel leaned forward, murmuring in her ear, 'Close your eyes. I won't touch you, just imagine...'

Here, alone with him on a windy hilltop, warmed by the crackling flames of a fire, Flora could do that. She could leave her anger behind, along with everything that stood between them, and visualise his kiss and the feel of his fingers tracing her skin. She shivered with pleasure, opening her eyes again.

'You're smiling.' He was smiling too. The knowledge that he'd been watching her face, knowing that she was thinking of him, sent tingles of sensuality down her spine.

'That was a great kiss. One of the best.'

He raised his eyebrows. 'So we kissed? I'm glad you liked it. Any chance I might get to participate in the next one?'

He was closer now, and Flora closed her eyes again. This time she didn't have to imagine the feel of his lips on hers. They were tender at first, like the brush of a feather, and when she responded to him the kiss deepened. She grabbed the front of his jacket, pulling him close, and felt his arms wrap around her.

Arousal hit her hard. The kind of physical

yearning that she'd searched for so many times and which had eluded her. It was impossible to be cold with Aksel.

'That was much better. There are some things I can't imagine all on my own.'

He grinned suddenly. 'I liked it much better, too.'

'Would you like…to continue this? Somewhere more comfortable?'

'Will you promise me one thing?' He hesitated.

'What's that?'

'Don't fake it with me, Flora. However this turns out is okay, but I need you to be honest with me.'

She stretched up, kissing his cheek. 'No secrets, no lies. It's what I want, too.'

The thought that Flora had trusted him enough to feel that this time might be different was both a pleasure and a challenge. Aksel kicked earth onto the smouldering remains of the fire and shouldered his backpack, holding her hand to guide her down the steepest part of the hill, which led most directly to her cottage.

Flora unlocked her front door, stepping inside and turning to meet his gaze when he didn't follow her.

'Have you changed your mind?'

'No. But it's okay for you to change yours. At any time.'

She replied by pulling him inside and kicking the door shut behind them, then stretching up to kiss him. It was impossible that she didn't feel the electricity that buzzed between them and when she gave a little gasp of pleasure, unzipping his jacket so that they could nuzzle closer, it felt dizzyingly arousing. He wanted her so badly, and she seemed to want him. The thought that he might not be able to please her as he wanted to clawed suddenly at his heart.

Maybe he shouldn't take that too personally. Flora had been quick enough to tell him that he wasn't in charge of everything that happened around him. He would be a kind and considerate lover, and if things didn't work out the way they wanted, he'd try not to be paralysed by guilt.

'I'll love you the best that I can…' The urgent promise tore from his lips.

'I know you will. That's all I want.' She took his hand and led him up the stairs.

CHAPTER FOURTEEN

He was letting her dictate the pace. Caught between urgent passion and nagging fear, Flora had no idea what she wanted that pace to be. Aksel pulled back the patchwork quilt that covered her bed and sat down, waiting for her to come to him.

She opened the wooden box that stood on top of the chest of drawers, rummaging amongst the collection of single earrings and pieces of paper that she shouldn't lose. Right at the bottom, she found the packet of condoms.

'I have these. I hope they're not out of date…' Her laugh sounded shrill and nervous.

'Let's see.' He held out his hand, and she dropped the packet into it. Aksel examined it carefully and then shot her a grin. 'They're okay for another six months.'

'Good. Maybe we'll save one for later.' The joke didn't sound as funny as she'd hoped. In fact, it sounded stupid and needy, but his slow smile never wavered.

Aksel caught her hand, pressing it to his lips. She sank down onto his knee and he embraced her, kissing her again, and suddenly there was only him. Undressing her slowly. Allowing him to patiently explore all the things that pleased her was going to be a long journey, full of many delights.

'Stop…' She'd let out a sigh of approval when he got to the fourth button of her shirt, and he paused, laying his finger across her lips. 'Be still. Be quiet, for as long as you can.'

'How will you know the difference?' In Flora's rather limited experience, most men wanted as much affirmation as they could get.

He gave a small shrug. 'If I don't know the difference when I hear it, then I really shouldn't be here.'

Flora put her arms possessively around his neck. This guy was *not* going anywhere. And if he wanted her to fight the rising passion until there was no choice but to give in to it, then that was what she would do.

She kept silent, even though her limbs were shaking as he undressed her. The touch of his skin against hers almost made her cry out, but she swallowed the sound. Flora had never had a man attend to her pleasure so assiduously before, and while the physical effect of that was evident in the growing hunger she felt, the emotional effect was far more potent.

He moved back onto the bed, sitting up against the pillows, and lifting her astride him. Face to face, both able to see and touch wherever they pleased. She reached round to the nape of his neck, undoing the band that was tied around his hair, and letting it fall forward.

'Is that what you want?' He smiled suddenly.

'Yes.' She kissed him again. 'I want that too.'

Aksel laughed softly. 'What else?'

It was an impossible question. 'It's too long a list. I don't think I know where to start...'

'How about here, then?'

She felt his arm coil around her back, pulling her against his chest. His other hand covered her breast, and she felt the brush of his hair against her shoulder as he kissed her neck. Flora closed her eyes, trying to contain her excitement.

She couldn't help it. Her own ragged cry took

her by surprise. Wordless, unmodulated, it was as if Mother Nature had climbed in through a window and stripped away everything but instinct and pleasure. She felt Aksel harden, as if this was what he'd been waiting for. If she'd known that it would feel so good, she'd have been waiting for it too.

'I want you so much, Flora…'

But he was going to wait until she was ready. Flora reached for the condoms, her hands shaking. When she touched him, to roll one on, she saw his eyes darken suddenly, an involuntary reaction that told her that he too was fighting to keep the last vestiges of control.

When she lifted her body up and took him inside, Aksel groaned, his head snapping back. And his large gentle hands spread across her back.

This time things were going to be different. No faking it, and… No thought either. She was thinking too much. Flora felt herself tremble in his arms, returning his kisses as the tension built. A soft, rolling tide that must surely grow.

He sensed it too. The fragile, tingling feeling rose and then dissipated, leaving her shaken but still unsatisfied. All the same, it was something. More than she'd experienced for a long time.

Aksel didn't question her, but as he held her against his chest she could hear his heartbeat. He wanted to know.

'It was nice… Something.'

'Not everything, though?' His chest heaved, with the same disappointment that Flora felt. Nagging frustration turned once more to hunger.

'Can we try again?' He was still inside her. Flora knew that he must feel that hunger too.

'Maybe we should stop. I don't want to hurt you.'

'You won't. I want to try again, and this time I…don't want you to be so gentle.'

He hesitated. Flora knew that she was asking a lot of him. *Just take me. Make me come.* Maybe that was too much weight of expectation to put on any man.

But she knew that he wanted to. She wriggled out of his arms, moving away from him. Bound now only by gaze.

'Don't you want me?'

'Are you crazy, Flora? You're everything any

man could want, and far more than I have a right to take…'

'But I'm asking you to do it anyway.'

For one moment, she thought he'd turn away from her. And then he moved, so quickly that he'd caught her up and pinned her down on the bed before she knew quite what was happening. His eyes were dark, tender and fierce all at the same time.

'Take my hand.' His elbows were planted on either side of her, and she reached up, feeling his fingers curl around hers in what seemed a lot like a promise. Whatever happened next, he'd be right there with her.

They'd faced passion together, and then faced disappointment. The kind of disappointment that a man—Aksel, anyway—found difficult to forget. If Flora hadn't already given him a good talking to about the nature of guilt, he'd be feeling far too responsible, and much too guilty to do this.

But when he'd tipped her onto her back, she'd gasped with delight, smiling up at him and putting her hand in his when he asked her. Trapped in her gaze, entering her for the second time was even better than the first. Better than anything he'd ever done, and it felt liable to overshadow anything he ever *would* do again.

She wrapped her legs around his back, and he felt her skin against his, warm and welcoming. He began to move, and her eyes darkened as her pupils dilated. Her body responded to his, a thin sheen of perspiration forming on her brow.

Aksel watched her carefully, revelling in all the little signs of her arousal. Suddenly she gasped, her whole body quivering for a moment in anticipation and her hand gripping his tightly. And then that sweet, sweet feeling as Flora clung to him, choking out his name.

It broke him. His own orgasm tore through him, leaving him breathless, his heart hammering in his chest. When he was able to focus his eyes again, the one thing he'd most wanted was right in front of him.

'You're smiling.'

Flora reached up, her fingertips caressing the side of his face. 'So are you.'

'Yes.' Aksel had the feeling that it was one of those big, stupid after-sex smiles. One that nothing in this world could wipe from his face. 'I'm not even going to ask. I know you weren't faking that.'

The thought seemed to please her. As if she'd wanted him to feel the force of her orgasm, without having to be told.

'I loved it. Every moment.'

'I loved it too.'

Her hand was still in his, and he raised it to his lips, kissing her fingers. Easing away from her for a moment, he arranged the pillows and she snuggled against him, laying her head on his chest, so soft and warm in his arms. Aksel let out a sigh of absolute contentment.

Flora had slept soundly, and she woke before dawn. The clock on the bedside table glowed the numbers six and twelve in the darkness. Twelve minutes past six was more Aksel's wake-up call than it was hers.

But he was still asleep. And she felt wide awake and more ready to meet the day than she usually did at this time in the morning.

She moved, stretching her limbs, and his eyelids fluttered open. Those blue eyes, the ones that had taken her to a place she'd been afraid to go last night.

Afraid... The clarity of early morning thoughts wondered whether it might just be the case that she'd been afraid all these years. Afraid to give herself to a man who didn't trust her enough for her to trust him back.

But she'd given herself to Aksel. In one overwhelming burst of passion that really should have been accompanied by booming cannons, waving flags, and perhaps a small earthquake. And she couldn't help smiling every time she thought about it.

He stretched, and she felt the smooth ripple of muscle. Then he reached for her hand, the way he had last night. He was still here, with her. Still protecting her from the doubts and fears.

'God morgen.' He leaned over, kissing her brow.

He'd lapsed into Norwegian a few times last night as they'd lain curled together in the darkness. It was as if his thoughts didn't wait to be translated before they reached his tongue, and although Flora didn't know what he'd said, the way he'd said it had left her in no doubt. They had been words of love, whispered in the quiet warmth of an embrace, and meant to be felt rather than heard.

'Are you…?' Did he feel as good as she did? Did he want this moment to last before the day began to edge it out? Flora couldn't think of a way of saying that in any language.

He chuckled, flexing his limbs again. 'I am. Are you?'

'Yes. I am too.'

All she needed was to lie here with him, holding his hand. But the sound of paws scrabbling at the kitchen door broke the silence.

'That's Dougal. He won't stop until I let him out…' Flora reluctantly tried to disentangle herself from Aksel's embrace, but he held on to her.

'I'll go. If you'd like to stay here, then I'll make you some breakfast.'

That would be nice, but even the time it took to make a couple of pieces of toast would be too long an absence. Flora let go of his hand and sat up. Even that was too much distance and she bent to kiss him again.

'I'll go. Are you hungry?'

He shook his head. 'Coffee or juice would be nice.'

She could let Dougal out, give him some food and water, and make coffee in two minutes flat if she hurried. 'Will you still be naked when I get back?'

Aksel grinned. 'You can count on it.'

She took the road into the estate as fast as the freezing morning would allow, and dropped Aksel off at the therapy centre at ten to nine, leaving him to take Dougal inside. If anyone noticed, then giving a next-door neighbour a lift into work couldn't excite any comment. She made it up to her office at one minute to nine, tearing off her coat and sitting down at her desk. Her first session of the morning wasn't until half past nine, and she could at least look as if she was at work, even though her mind was elsewhere.

Her whole body felt different, as if it was still bathed in Aksel's smile. Science told her that it was probably the effect of feel-good neuro-transmitters and hormones, but rational thought had its limitations. Aksel seemed to have no limitations at all.

When she closed her eyes, she could still feel him. He'd brushed off her suggestion that surely there wasn't anything more he might explore, and had taken her on a sensory journey that had proved her wrong. Aksel made foreplay into an exquisite art, and he obviously enjoyed it just as much as she did.

'Flora, we've a new patient....' Her eyes snapped open again to see Charles Ross-Wylde staring at her from the doorway. 'Are you all right?'

'Oh. Yes, I'm fine. Just concentrating.' Flora wondered if it looked as if she'd just spent two hours having stupendous sex. In the three years she'd been here, she'd never seen Charles show any interest in anything other than work, and he might not understand.

'Yes. Of course. As long as you're not feeling unwell.'

'No!' She could have sounded a little less emphatic about that as Charles was beginning to look puzzled. Best get down to business. 'You've a new patient for me to see…?'

The day wasn't without its victories. Andy Wallace had mentioned that Aksel had popped in, bringing Mette with him, and that they'd talked about ice carving and the long road that led across the Andes. The friendship seemed to have given Andy the final push to take his first step unaided.

Flora had tried to conceal her blushes when Andy had talked about Aksel, but he was in the habit of watching everyone closely. When they'd finished their session together, Andy had asked her to give Aksel his best when she saw him, smiling quietly when Flora had said she would.

Dougal seemed a little calmer when she picked him up from the centre, and didn't make his usual frenetic dash around the cottage. He lay down in front of the fire, growling quietly.

'What's the matter, Dougal?' Flora bent down to stroke him, and he gave her his usual response, his tail thumping against the hearth. She walked into the kitchen, wondering if he'd follow, and he bounded past her, pawing at the cupboard where she kept his food. Whatever it was, it didn't seem to have affected his appetite.

She knew that Aksel would come. He'd be late, staying at the clinic until Mette was ready to go to bed, but he'd come. She heard the sound of the battered SUV outside, and smiled. He usually walked back from the castle, but tonight he was in a hurry.

The doorbell rang and she opened the door. Aksel was leaning against the opening of the porch, grinning.

'Are you coming in?'

'Are you going to ask me in?' There didn't seem to be any doubt in his mind that she would.

'Since you're holding a bottle of wine, then yes.'

He stepped inside, and Flora took the bottle from his hand, putting it down on the hall table. Without giving him the chance to take off his coat, she kissed him.

'I thought you wanted the wine,' he teased her, kissing her again hungrily.

'Isn't that just an excuse? To call round?'

'Yes, it's an excuse. Although if you'd prefer to just sit around the fire and drink it...' Aksel seemed determined to give her the choice, even though their kisses had already shown that neither of them wanted to spend the rest of evening anywhere else than in bed.

'No. I want you stone-cold sober. Upstairs.'

Aksel chuckled. 'I'll have you stone-cold sober, too. And calling out my name, the way you did last night.'

The thought was almost too much, but there was still something she had to do. Dougal was lying in front of the fire, still making those odd growling sounds.

'Will you take a look at Dougal first?'

'Of course. What's the matter with him?' Aksel walked into the sitting room, bending down to greet Dougal.

'I'm not sure. He's eating fine, and he doesn't seem to be in any pain. But he's making these odd noises.'

Aksel nodded, trying to stop Dougal from licking him as he examined him. Then he nodded in satisfaction. 'There's absolutely nothing wrong with him. He's trying to purr.'

'What?' That didn't sound like much of a diagnosis. 'Like a cat?'

'Yes.' Aksel tickled Dougal behind his ears and he rolled on his back, squirming in delight and growling. 'When I arrived at work this morning, I went to the office to finish up my report for Esme on the dog visiting scheme. I took Dougal with me to keep him out of the way as everyone was busy.'

'And you have a cat in the office at the canine therapy centre? Isn't that a bit of an explosive mix?'

Aksel shrugged, getting to his feet. 'Cats and dogs aren't necessarily natural enemies. A dog's instinct is to chase smaller animals, and a cat's instinct is to sense that as an attack, and flee. It's all a big misunderstanding, really.'

'Okay, so there was a cat at the centre...'

'Yes, someone brought it in, thinking that they might take it. Esme wasn't about to turn it away because... Esme doesn't know *how* to turn an animal in need away. And Dougal's natural instinct seems to be to make friends with everything that moves, and so by the end of the morning the two of them were curled up together. The cat was purring away and Dougal... I guess he was just trying to make friends.'

'So now we've got a dog that thinks he's a cat on our hands.' Flora looked down at Dougal, and he trotted up to her, rubbing his head against her leg.

'Maybe he'll grow out of it.'

Maybe. It made the little dog even more loveable, if that was at all possible. And talking of loveable…

'So… Mette and Kari are at the castle, and they're both fast asleep by now. Dougal's okay, apart from a few minor identity issues.' She approached Aksel, reaching up to wrap her arms around his neck. 'That just leaves you and me.'

'And more than twelve hours before it's time to go back to work.' Aksel grinned, and picked her up in his arms.

CHAPTER FIFTEEN

THEY LAY ON the bed together, naked. Aksel had made love to her, and each time he did, it was more mind-blowing than the last. Things were going to have to plateau at some point, or Flora's nerve endings were going to fry.

'You know, don't you? When someone you're with has an orgasm.' Flora wondered whether the other guys she'd been with had known too. Maybe they had, and just hadn't cared.

'I do with you.' He grinned lazily. 'I suppose you want to know how.'

Yes, she did. Very much, because it seemed to please him so much. 'Tell me.'

'Your pupils dilate. You start to burn up, and you cry out for me. Then your muscles start to contract...'

'You like that?' Flora traced her fingertips across the ripple of muscles in his chest.

'You know I do. And you can't fake any of that.'

'Strictly speaking… I think you could try.'

'No, you wouldn't fool me.' Aksel curled his arm around her, pulling her a little closer. 'What we have is honesty, and I'd know if that ever changed.'

It was a good answer. They *were* honest with each other. It had been something that had just happened from day one. Perhaps it was that which had guided them past all the traps and obstacles, and led them here.

'Well, honestly…' Flora propped herself up on one arm so that she could look into his eyes '…you are the most perfect, beautiful man I've ever seen.'

He didn't believe that. Aksel thought that his body was a workhorse that got him from one place to another, along with anything he carried with him. Vanity didn't occur to him.

'I'd urge you to make an appointment with your optician if you think I'm perfect.'

'You have a great body. *Very* nice arms.'

'Uneven toes…' He wiggled the toes on his left foot, two of which had been amputated above the distal phalangeal joint.

'Not very uneven. You only lost the tips of your toes, and they tell a story.'

'One that I won't forget in a hurry. Frost-bite's painful.'

'And the mark on your arm?'

'That's where I was bitten by a snake. In South America.'

'And this one?' Flora ran her finger across a scar on his side.

'I was in a truck that tipped over while fording a river. The current turned out to be a bit stronger than we anticipated.'

'And you have a couple of small lumps along your clavicle where you broke it. The muscles in your shoulders are a little tight because you worry. A little tension in your back because Mette loves it when you carry her on your shoulders. Most people's bodies reflect who they are, and how they've lived, and yours is perfect.'

'And you… You really *are* perfect, Flora. You're made of warmth and love, and that makes you flawlessly beautiful.' He chuckled. 'Apart from that little scar on your knee.'

'It's not as good a story as yours are. I fell off my bike when I was a kid.'

Aksel reached up, pulling her down for a

kiss. 'It's a great story. The scar's charming, along with the rest of you.'

Flora ran her fingers through his hair. Thick and blond, most women would kill for hair like that.

'Okay…so what's with the hair, then?' He knew that she liked it spread over his shoulders, instead of tied back, especially when they made love.

'It makes you look free, like a wild creature. Is that why you grew it so long?'

He shrugged. 'I don't know. Maybe I just never got around to cutting it. I like the sound of that, though.'

She kissed him again. 'Don't get around to cutting it, Aksel. That's perfect too.'

Aksel was happy. He felt free when he made love to Flora. And even when they weren't making love, the contentment that he felt whenever he was in her company was making him feel that maybe there was a little life left in his battered, careworn heart.

Tonight he'd be sleeping apart from Flora, though. He'd arranged to bring Mette home for the afternoon, and she'd stay the night with him at the cottage, before returning to the clinic the next morning. It had gone without saying that this was something that he needed to do alone.

He'd decided on some games, and had bought all of Mette's favourite foods. When he arrived home with her, he spread the colourful quilt on her bed, walking her around the cottage to remind her of the layout.

Everything just clicked into place, as if he'd been there all of Mette's life. She enjoyed her afternoon, and dozed in his arms as he told her the story about how crocodiles and penguins had helped him to reach the top of a high mountain in safety.

'I want to say goodnight to Mama.'

Aksel realised suddenly that in his determination to get everything right, he'd forgotten all about Mette's electric candle and had left it by her bed at the clinic. But it was important that his daughter felt she could speak to her mother whenever she wanted to. He reached for one of the Christmas candles that Flora had arranged on his mantelpiece, putting it into the grate.

'We'll use Tante Flora's candle, shall we? Just for tonight.'

Mette nodded, and Aksel fetched matches

from the kitchen and lit the candle. They sat together on the hearthrug, saying their goodnights, and Mette leaned forward and blew out the candle. Aksel carried her upstairs, settled her into her bed and kissed her goodnight.

At a loose end now, and not wanting to go downstairs just yet in case Mette stirred, he went to his own bedroom and lay down on the bed, staring at the ceiling. This was the first night that he'd been completely alone with her, and it was a responsibility that brought both happiness and a measure of terror.

Aksel woke up to the feeling of something tugging at his arm. Opening his eyes, he realised that Kari had hold of his sweater in her jaws and was pulling as hard as she could to make him wake up and get off the bed. A moment later the smoke alarm started to screech a warning that made his blood run cold.

'Mette...' He catapulted himself off the bed and into her room. The bedclothes were drawn to one side and Mette was nowhere to be seen. Remembering that children had a habit of hiding when they sensed danger, he wrenched open the wardrobe doors, but she wasn't there either.

As he ran downstairs, he could smell smoke, but he couldn't see where it was coming from. Mette was curled up at the bottom of the stairs, crying, and he picked her up, quickly wrapped her in his coat, then opened the front door and ran with her to the end of the path.

'Papa. Kari made me go away from the fire.'

Cold remorse froze his heart suddenly. He could see a flicker of flame through the sitting-room window. Kari must have herded Mette out of danger, shutting the door behind them as she'd been taught. He held his daughter close, feeling tears run down his face.

'It's all right, Mette. Everything's all right. You're safe…'

The sound of an alarm beeping somewhere woke Flora up. It wasn't coming from inside the cottage, and she rolled drowsily out of bed, sliding her feet into her slippers and peering out of the window. She saw Aksel outside with Mette in his arms, Kari sitting obediently at his feet.

Running downstairs, she grabbed her coat, not stopping to put it on. As soon as she was outside, the faint smell of smoke hit her and she hurried over to Aksel.

'Are you both all right?'

He raised his face towards her, and Flora saw tears. Mette realised that she was there, although she must be practically blind in the darkness, and reached out from the warm cradle of his arms.

'Papa says we're safe.' Aksel seemed too overwhelmed to speak, and Mette volunteered the information.

'That's right. You're safe now.'

She looked up at Aksel questioningly, and he brushed his hand across his face. 'There's a fire, I think it's pretty much contained to the sitting room. Will you take Mette while I go and have a look.'

'No, Aksel. Wait for the fire brigade. Have you called them?'

'My phone's inside. Please, take her.'

It seemed that Aksel was more comfortable with dealing with the situation than he was with taking care of his daughter right now. Flora wondered how the fire had started. She took Mette, holding the little girl tight in her arms.

'Papa's just looking to see how big the fire

is.' As Aksel walked back up the path, peering through the front windows, Mette craned round to keep him in view.

'It's all right, he's quite safe. He isn't getting too close, so the fire won't burn him.'

Mette seemed more confident of that than Flora felt. 'My papa fights crocodiles.'

'There you are, then. If he can fight crocodiles then a little fire will be easy…'

She watched, holding her breath as Aksel walked back towards them, his face set in a look of grim determination.

'It's just the hearth rug at the moment. Will you look after Mette while I go and put it out?'

'You should leave it, until the fire brigade gets here. We'll go inside and call them now…'

'I can put it out, there's a fire extinguisher in the kitchen. And if we leave it, then it may spread to the chimney. I don't know how long it's been since it's been swept, and I want to avoid that.'

A chimney fire could easily spread to her cottage. Flora dismissed the thought. What mattered was that they were all safe. 'No, Aksel…'

He was going anyway. She may as well accept it, and work with what was inevitable. Flora transferred Mette into his arms for a moment while she wriggled out of her own coat, wrapping it around the little girl so that his was no longer needed.

'If you must go, put your coat on, it'll protect your arms. And put a pair of boots on as well.'

He looked down at his feet, seeming to realise for the first time that he was only wearing a pair of socks. 'Okay. You're right. You'll take Mette inside?'

She was shivering, her pyjamas giving no protection against the wind. But she wasn't moving until she saw that Aksel was safe. 'If you must go, go now. Before the fire gets any worse. And no heroics, Aksel. Back off if it looks to be getting worse.'

He nodded. Giving Kari a curt command, he strode back up the path, opening the door to his cottage.

Kari was on the alert now, sniffing the air and looking around. Aksel had clearly ordered the dog to protect them, and she was taking her task seriously. Flora hugged Mette close, pulling her coat down around the child's feet.

'Papa's just going to put out the fire. He won't

be a minute.' She said the words as if it was nothing. Maybe it *was* nothing to Aksel, but right now it seemed a great deal to her.

She watched as Aksel's dark figure approached the fire. A plume of shadows emitted from the fire extinguisher and the flames died almost immediately. He disappeared for a moment and then reappeared with a bucket, tipping its contents over the ashes to make sure that the fire was well and truly out.

Okay. Everything was okay, and now all she wanted to do was to get warm. By the time Aksel reappeared her teeth were chattering.

'Everything all right?'

'No.' He took his coat off and wrapped it around her. 'You're freezing.'

'The fire's out, though…' He was hurrying her towards her own front door, his arm around her shoulders.

'Yes. I made sure of it.' Aksel pushed the door open and glorious warmth surrounded her suddenly. 'Come and sit down.'

He was gentle and attentive, but his eyes were dead. Whatever he felt was locked behind an impervious barrier.

'Stay with Mette and I'll make a hot drink.' Flora was trying to stop shivering.

'No, I'll do that. You sit and get warm.' He picked up the woollen blanket that was folded across the back of the sofa and waited until Flora had sat down, then tucked it around her and Mette. Then he disappeared into the kitchen.

He came back with two cups of tea, and Flora drank hers while he went upstairs to the bathroom to wash his hands and face. When he came back and sat down, Mette crawled across the sofa, snuggling against him and yawning. Flora waited for the little girl to fall asleep before she asked the inevitable question.

'What happened?'

'I was asleep upstairs. Kari and Mette were downstairs, and Kari herded Mette out into the hallway and shut the door. Then she came to wake me up.' He held out his hand, and Kari ambled over to him. He fondled the dog's ears and she laid her head in his lap.

'You taught her to do that?'

He nodded. 'I didn't even know that Mette was out of bed.'

'What was she doing downstairs?'

'From the looks of it, she'd gone downstairs and lit a candle in the grate. It must have fallen over onto the hearth rug...' His voice cracked and broke with emotion.

'Where did she get the matches from?' Aksel had clearly already tried and convicted himself, without even listening to the case for the defence.

'They were in one of the high cupboards in the kitchen. I didn't think she could get to them, but when I went back inside I saw that she'd dragged a chair across the room. She must have climbed up on it, then got up onto the counter top and into the cupboard.'

It was quite an achievement for a six-year-old with poor sight. 'What made her so determined to light a candle in the middle of the night?' Flora's hand flew to her mouth. She knew the answer.

'When I packed her things, I forgot her electric candle. So I lit a real one for her. It's all my...' He fell silent as Flora flapped her hand urgently at him.

'Don't. You're not to say it. It's *not* your fault.'

'That's not borne out by the facts.' His face

was blank, as if he'd accepted his guilt without any question.

Flora took a breath. Whatever she said now had to be convincing. 'Look, Aksel, I talk to a lot of parents in the course of my work. The one thing that everyone agrees on is that you can't watch your children twenty-four hours a day. It isn't possible. But you've come up with a good second-best, and you trained Kari to watch over her.'

He narrowed his eyes. 'You're just making excuses for me.'

'No, I'm not. You let her say goodnight to her mother, Aksel, she needs to do that. And you put the matches away, somewhere that should have been out of her reach.'

'She *did* reach them, though.'

'Well, you might be able to take part of the blame for that one. She takes after her father in being resourceful. I imagine she has all kinds of challenges up her sleeve…'

'All right. You're making me panic now.'

If he didn't like that, then he *really* wasn't going to like the next part. 'You need to let her know, Aksel, that she mustn't play with matches.'

He sighed. 'Yes. I know. Her grandmother always told her off when she was naughty...'

'Yeah, right. You can't rely on her to be the bad guy now.'

Right on cue, Mette shifted fitfully in his arms, opening her eyes. 'Papa, the fire's out?'

'Yes.'

'Did you save all the crocodiles, and the penguins?' Mette was awake again now, and probably ready to play. Aksel's face took on an agonised look, knowing that the time had come for him to be the bad guy.

'Yes, the crocodiles and penguins are all fine. Mette, there's something I have to say to you.'

Mette's gaze slid guiltily towards Flora and she struggled not to react. Aksel had to do this by himself.

'I love you very much, Mette, and you know that you can talk to Mama any time you want.' He started with the positive. 'But you mustn't touch matches or light candles when I'm not there. And you mustn't climb up onto cupboards either. You could hurt yourself very badly.'

A large tear rolled down Mette's cheek. Flora could almost see Aksel's heart breaking.

'Is the fire my fault, Papa?'

'No. It's my fault. I didn't tell you not to do those things, and I should have. But I want you to promise not to do them again.' He waited a moment for Mette to respond. 'You have to say it, please, Mette. "I promise…"'

Mette turned the corners of her mouth down in a look of abject dismay. Even Flora wanted to forgive her immediately, and she wondered whether getting to the North Pole had presented quite as much of a challenge to Aksel as this.

'I promise, Papa.' Another tear rolled down her cheek and Aksel nodded.

'Thank you.' Finally he broke, cuddling Mette to his chest. 'I love you very much.'

'I love you too, Papa.'

'What was it you wanted to say to Mama?' He kissed the top of his daughter's head.

'I forgot to tell her all about our house. And that I like my room…'

'All right. We'll go back to the clinic and find your candle. And you can tell Mama all about it.'

'When?'

'Right now, Mette.'

Mette nodded, satisfied with his answer, and curled up in his arms, her eyelids drooping again drowsily. Flora handed him the woollen blanket and he wrapped his daughter in it, leaving her to sleep. Finally his gaze found Flora's.

'Forget wrestling crocodiles. That was the most difficult thing...'

'*Have* you wrestled a crocodile?'

'Actually, no. Mette thinks I have, but that's not as dangerous as it sounds because she thinks that her cuddly crocodile is a true-to-life representation. I tell her a story about crocodiles and penguins that I met when I was in the Andes.'

'Right. Even I could wrestle a cuddly toy. I didn't know there were crocodiles in the Andes.'

'There aren't. She added a few things in as we went along. The penguins act as tour guides and show you the right way to go.'

'Penguins are always the good guys.'

He nodded, finally allowing himself a smile. 'I'm going to take her back to the clinic, now.'

'What? It's three in the morning, Aksel. Why don't you just stay here?'

'I said that we'd go now so that she can talk to Lisle. And I want her to wake up somewhere that's familiar to her.'

'But…' Flora saw the logic of it but this felt wrong. 'She's asleep. It seems a shame to take her out into the cold now when you can let her sleep and take her back first thing in the morning.'

'You heard me promise her, Flora. I'll stay the night so that I'll be there whenever she wakes up. You can't help me with this.'

There was more to this than just practicality. More than a promise. She could feel Aksel slipping away from her, torn by his guilt and the feeling that he'd let his daughter down.

Flora had to let him go. He'd feel differently about this in the morning and realise that he could be a father to Mette and a lover to her as well.

'Okay. You'll be back in the morning?'

'Yes.' He reached for her, and Flora slid towards him on the sofa. His kiss was tender, but it held none of the fire of their nights together.

'You're tired. You'll sleep in?'

If she could sleep at all. Dread began to pulse through her. What if he decided that this was where their relationship had to end? She pushed the thought away. She *had* to trust Aksel. There was no other choice.

'I'll phone in and take a couple of hours off work, I don't have any patients to see in the morning. I'll be here when you get back.'

He nodded. 'I'll come as soon as I can.'

CHAPTER SIXTEEN

FLORA WAS UP early and let herself into Aksel's cottage with the spare key that he'd left with her. The place stank of smoke, and there were deposits of soot all around the sitting room, but apart from that the damage was relatively minor. She tidied the kitchen, putting away the evidence of Mette having climbed up to reach the matches, and tipped the remains of the hearth rug into a rubbish bag. Then she brewed a cup of strong coffee to jolt her tired and aching limbs into action and started to clean.

Ten minutes after she'd returned to her own cottage for more coffee and some breakfast, Flora heard the throaty roar of the SUV outside in the lane. Running out to embrace him seemed as if it would only make the awful what-ifs of last night a reality again, and she forced herself to sit down at the kitchen table and wait for him to come to her.

When he did, he looked as tired as she felt. But the first thing he did, when she let him into the cottage, was hug her. His body seemed stiff and unresponsive, but it was still a hug. Things were going to be all right.

'I appreciate the clean-up, but I was hoping to find you'd slept in this morning.' He sat down at the kitchen table while she made him coffee.

'Your early mornings are starting to rub off on me.' It wouldn't do to tell him she'd been awake most of the night, worrying. Normal was good at the moment, even if she was going to have to fake it.

She put his coffee down in front of him and sat down. 'So how's Mette?'

'Fine. She told me that a fire's a very second-league adventure. Fighting crocodiles is much more exciting.' He smiled suddenly, and Flora laughed.

'Shame. If we could have tempted a few out of the loch then you could have done that too.'

He laughed, but there was no humour in his eyes. They were going through the motions of believing in life again, without any of the certainty.

'Aksel, I… What happened last night was a terrible accident. Mette's all right and so are you.'

'Yes. I know.' He might know it, but he didn't seem to believe it.

'You're a good father. You can keep her safe. We'll do it together, we'll go through the whole cottage and check everything… We can learn from this and make sure that it doesn't happen again.'

He looked at her blankly. 'We?'

'Yes, *we.* You're not alone with this, we'll do it together.'

'*I* need to do it, Flora. When I go back to Oslo…' They both knew what happened then. When he went back to Oslo, she would stay here in Cluchlochry, and it would be an end to their relationship. Aksel couldn't bring himself to rely on her.

She'd thought about this. It was far too early to say anything, but maybe it needed to be said now. Maybe they both needed to know that their relationship didn't have to be set in stone, and that it did have a future.

'When you go back to Oslo, there's nothing

to stop me from visiting, is there?' Flora decided to start slowly with this.

He looked up at her. The look in his eyes told Flora that maybe she hadn't started slowly enough.

'I just... It seems so very arbitrary, to put an end date on this. What we have.'

'We'll always have it, Flora. There's no end date on that.'

It was a nice thought. A romantic thought, which didn't bear examination. Over time, the things they'd shared would be tarnished and forgotten.

'That's not what I meant. I was thinking in a more...literal sense.' Flora's heart began to beat fast. This wasn't going quite the way she'd hoped, and she was beginning to dread what Aksel might say.

'You're thinking of coming to Norway?'

'Well... I'm a free agent. I can come and see you, can't I?'

This wasn't about Mette any more. It was about Aksel's determination to do things on his own. About hers to find someone who trusted her. It was a bright winter morning, warm and cosy inside with snow falling outside the window, but Flora could feel the chill now, instead of the heat.

He was still and silent for a moment. When he looked at her, Flora could only see the mountain man, doggedly trudging forward, whatever the cost. Whatever he left behind.

'Do you seriously think that if you came to Norway, I'd ever let you go?'

Flora swallowed hard. That sounded like a *no*.

'Okay.' She shrugged, as if it didn't matter to her. 'That's okay, I won't come, then.'

'Flora...' He reached across the table, laying his hand on her arm. The sudden warmth in his eyes only made her angry and she pulled away from him.

'I heard what you said, Aksel.' He didn't want her. Actually, not wanting her would have been relatively okay. Flora knew that he wanted her but that he was fighting it.

'I didn't mean...' He let out a breath, frustration showing in his face. Clearly he didn't know quite what he meant. Or maybe he did, and he wasn't going to say it. In a moment of horrible clarity Flora knew exactly what he meant.

Aksel wouldn't take the risk of things becoming permanent between them. She'd trusted him, and he was pushing her away now. They'd tried to be happy—and surely they both deserved it. But Aksel was going to turn his back on that and let her down.

'Don't worry about it. I know what you're saying to me. That you're in control of this, and it comes to an end when you go. Well, I'm taking control of it and it ends now. I'm going to work.'

'Flora…' he called after her, but Flora had already walked out of the kitchen. Pulling on her coat, she picked up Dougal's lead, which was all she needed to do to prompt him to scrabble at the front door.

He'd made her feel him. He'd been inside her, in more ways than just physically, and she'd dared to enjoy it. Dared to want more. When he caught her up in the hallway, and she turned to look at him, she still loved him. It would always be this way with Aksel, and she had to make the break now, for her own sanity's sake.

'Can't we talk about this?'

'I think we've said all we need to say, haven't we? If you see me again, just look the other way, Aksel. I don't want to speak to you, ever again.'

She pulled open the front door, slamming it in his face. Aksel would be gone by the time she got home from work this evening, and hopefully he'd take what she'd said seriously. If they saw each other in the village, or at the clinic, she'd be looking the other way, and so should he.

He'd messed up. Big time. Aksel had been in some very tight spots, but he couldn't remember one as terrifying and hopeless as this.

He'd spent most of the night sitting in the chair next to Mette's bed, staring into the darkness and wondering how he could make things right. How he could be a father to Mette, and love Flora as well. He'd come to no conclusion.

Last night's fire wasn't the issue. But it had shaken him and dredged up feelings that he'd struggled to bury. Lisle's lies. His guilt over not having been there for Mette. And when Flora had spoken of coming to Norway to visit...

He knew what she'd been doing. She'd been trying to patch things up and convince them both that nothing was the matter. Flora always tried to mend what was broken, and he loved her for it. But she deserved someone better than him. Now that he was responsible for Mette, could he ever be the man that Flora could trust?

The question hammered at him, almost driving him to his knees. He'd travelled a long way, and it had seemed that he'd finally found the thing that he hadn't even known he'd been looking for. Did he really have to turn his back on Flora? Aksel couldn't bear it, but if it had to be done, then it was better for it to be done now.

He took a gulp of his coffee, tipping the rest into the sink and clearing up the kitchen. Then he signalled to Kari to follow him out into the cold, crisp morning air. As Aksel shut Flora's front door behind him, he knew only two things for sure. That this hurt far more than anything he'd experienced before. And that now he had to go on the most important journey of his life. One that he'd told himself he'd never make, and which might just change everything.

Anger had propelled Flora through the morning. But anger was hard to sustain, particularly where Aksel was concerned. When she couldn't help thinking about his touch, the honesty in his clear blue eyes, and the way he gave himself to her...

But now he'd taken it all away. As the day wore on, each minute heavy on her hands, the sharp cutting edge of her fury gave way to a dull ache of pain. She hurried home after work, trying not to notice that his cottage was quiet and dark, no lights showing from the windows.

Flora spent a sleepless night, thinking what might have been, and wondering if a miracle might happen to somehow bring it all back again. The feeble light of morning brought her answer. It had been good between them, and Aksel was the man she'd always wanted. But he couldn't handle the guilt of feeling himself torn in two directions, and Flora couldn't handle trusting him and then having him push her away.

She'd decided that she must go and see Mette, because it wouldn't be fair to just desert the little girl. Making sure that Aksel wasn't at the clinic that morning, she spent an hour with Mette, putting on a happy face even though she was dying inside, and then went back to her treatment room, locking the door so that she could cry bitter tears.

It seemed that Aksel had got the message. He knew that she didn't want to see him, and he was avoiding her too. He was perceptive enough to know that things weren't going to work out between them, and it was better to break things off now. He might even be happy about that. Flora was a claim on his time and attention that he didn't need right now.

The second time she passed his cottage, on the way to her own front door, was no easier than the first. It looked as empty as it had last night, and Flora wondered whether he'd found somewhere else to stay.

But then she'd gone to the window to close the curtains and seen the light flickering at the top of the hill, partly obscured by the ruins of the old keep. Flora knew exactly where Aksel was now. This was his signal fire, and it was meant for her.

He might have just phoned... If Aksel had called her then she could have dismissed the call, and that would have been an end to it. But the fire at the top of the hill burned on, seeming to imprint itself on her retinas even when she wasn't staring out of the window at it.

She needed something to takc her mind off it. Her Christmas card list was always a good bet, and she fetched it, along with the boxes of cards that she'd bought, sitting down purposefully in front of the fire with a pen and a cup of tea. But her hand shook as she wrote. Wishing friends and family a happy Christmas always made her smile but, knowing that this year she'd be spending hers without Aksel, the Christmas greetings only emphasised her own hollow loneliness.

She gathered the cards up, deciding to leave them for another day. Drawing the curtains apart, she saw the light of the fire still twinkling out in the gloom…

Aksel had built the fire knowing that Flora would see it. And knowing that he'd stay here all night if he had to, and then the following night, and each night until she came. However long it took, he'd be here when Flora finally decided to climb the hill.

Maybe it wouldn't be tonight. It was getting late, and the lights of her cottage had been flicking on and off, tracing what seemed to be an irregular and undecided progress from room to room. Soon the on and off of the lights upstairs would signal that Flora had gone to bed, which left little chance that she'd come to him tonight.

All the same, he'd be here. Wrapped in his sleeping bag, until the first rays of dawn told him that he had to move now, work the cold stiffness from his limbs, and get on with another day.

His fire was burning low, and he went to fetch more fuel from the pile of branches that he'd stacked up nearby. The blaze began to climb through the dry twigs, brightening as it went, and he missed the one thing he had been waiting and watching for. When he looked down toward the village again, Flora's porch light was on.

He cursed his own inattentiveness, reaching for his backpack. His trembling fingers fumbled with the small binoculars, and he almost dropped them on the ground. Focussing them down towards Flora's cottage, he saw her standing in her porch, wearing her walking boots and thick, waterproof jacket, and looking up in his direction. Aksel almost recoiled, even though he knew that she couldn't see him. And then she went back inside the cottage again.

He bit back his disappointment. It had been too much to expect from this first night. But then she reappeared, pulling a hat onto her head, and as she started to walk away from the cottage a small thread of light issued from her hand. He smiled, glad that she'd remembered to bring a torch with her.

Aksel tried to calm himself by wondering which route she'd take. The most direct was the steepest, and it would be an easier walk to circle around the bottom of the hill before climbing it. She crossed the bridge that led from the village to the estate and disappeared for a moment behind a clump of bushes. And then he saw her again, climbing the steep, stony ground and making straight for him.

He waited, his eyes fixed on the small form labouring up the hill. When she fell, and the torch rolled skittishly back a few feet down the slope, he sprang to his feet, cursing himself for bringing her out here in the dark. But before he could run towards her, she was on her feet again, retrieving the torch.

Aksel forced himself to sit back down on the stony bench he'd made beside the fire. He *had* to wait, even though it was agony to watch Flora struggle like this. He had to trust that she'd come to him, and she had to know that she would too, however hard the journey.

His heart beat like a battering ram, and he suddenly found it difficult to breathe. The fire crackled and spat, flames flaring up into the night. The moment he'd longed for so desperately would be here soon, and despite working through every possible thing she might say to him, and what he might say in reply, he was completely unprepared.

When she finally made it to the top of the hill, she seemed rather too out of breath to say anything. Flora switched off her torch, putting her hands on her hips in a stance that indicated she wasn't going to take any nonsense from him.

'It's warmer by the fire...' He ventured the words and she frowned.

'This had better be good, Aksel. If you think I came up here in the middle of the night to hear something you might have said anywhere...'

'When might I have said it? You told me you never wanted to speak to me again.'

The logic had seemed perfect to him, but it only seemed to make her more angry. 'You could have slipped a note under my front door. It's not so far for either of us to walk.'

'I trusted you to come to me.'

She stared at him. 'I really wish you hadn't said that.'

Because it was the one thing he could have said to stop her from walking away from him? A sharp barb of hope bit into his heart.

'Sit down. Please.'

Flora pressed her lips together, hesitating for agonising moments. Then she marched over to the stone slab that he was sitting on, plumping herself down on the far end so that their shoulders didn't touch.

She was angry still, but at least she was sitting down. Aksel wasn't sure where to start, but before he could organise his thoughts, Flora did it for him.

'Where have you been, Aksel? You haven't been at the cottage and Mette told me that you weren't coming in to see her today.'

'You went to see Mette?' Of course she had.

Flora wouldn't let a little thing like a broken heart get in the way of making sure that a child wasn't hurt by her absence. And from the way that she seemed to hate him so much, Aksel was in no doubt that her heart was just as wounded as his.

'Yes. I made sure that you weren't there already.'

Good. Hate was a lot more akin to love than indifference was. 'I was in Oslo.'

'Oslo? For two days?'

'Just a day. I went to see Mette yesterday afternoon and left straight from there. I got back a couple of hours ago. The flight only takes an hour from Glasgow.'

She turned the edges of her mouth down. 'And it was such a long way when I was thinking of making the trip.'

He deserved that. 'I meant it when I said that I wouldn't be able to let you go, and that this is your home. I went to Oslo to talk with Olaf and Agnetha. About making this *my* home and Mette's.'

'You need their permission?' He could hear the fight beginning to go out of Flora's tone. She was starting to crumble, and if she wasn't in his arms yet, then maybe she would be if he gave it time.

'No, I don't. I'm Mette's father, and I make decisions about what's best for her, you taught me that. I wanted their blessing, and to reassure them that moving here didn't mean that they wouldn't get to see her.'

Flora stared at him. 'And...?'

'They told me that they expected me to get a house with a nice guest room, because they'll be visiting.'

A tear ran down her cheek. 'Aksel, please. What exactly are you saying?'

Now was the time. He had to be bold, because Flora couldn't be. He had to trust her, and show her that she could trust him. Aksel hung onto her hand for dear life.

'There's so much I want to say to you. But it all boils down to one thing.'

Flora had stumbled up a hill in the pitch darkness, and probably skinned her knees. If, in the process, she'd come to realise that nothing could keep her away from Aksel, she wanted to hear what he had to say for himself first.

The flickering flames bathed his face in

warmth, throwing the lines of worry across his forehead into sharp relief. The taut lines of his body showed that he was just as agitated as she was.

'What's the one thing?'

'I love you.'

That was good. It was very good because, despite herself, she loved him.

'Seriously?' Maybe he could be persuaded to say it again…

'Yes, seriously. I love you, Flora.' He was smiling at her in the firelight.

'I…love you too.'

He didn't argue. Putting his arms around her, he enveloped her in a hug.

'I was so horrible to you. I'm sorry, Aksel.' The things she'd said made Flora shiver now.

'You were afraid. I was afraid too, and our fear was all that we could see. But I'd be the bravest guy in the world if you'd just forgive me.'

'You mean I'm more scary than wrestling crocodiles?'

'Much more. But the thing that scares me most is losing you.'

Flora kissed him. So much nicer than words.

But even the wild pleasure of feeling him close, embraced in his fire on a cold, dark night, couldn't entircly wipe away the feeling that there were some things they really did need to talk about.

'Aksel... What if...?'

'What-ifs don't matter.' He kissed her again, and Flora broke away from him with an effort.

'They *do* matter, Aksel. I need to know. I want you to say it, because I can't keep wondering what might happen if we make a go of this, and decide to have children some day.'

'I'd like children very much. A boy, maybe. Or a girl. One or more of each would be more than acceptable...' He was grinning broadly now.

'Stop it! Don't even say that if you can't also say that there's a risk that one or more of our children might have cystic fibrosis.'

He took her hands between his. 'I know that there *may* be a risk, but only if I carry the gene as well. I love you and I trust you. It's not that I don't care about these possibilities, I just have no doubts that we can face it and do the right thing. And there are other things we need to do first.'

He trusted her. He'd take her as she was, with all the doubts that raised, and he'd make them into certainties. 'What other things do we need to do first?'

'First, I need to tell you that I intend to marry you. I'll work very hard towards making you so happy that you won't be able to resist asking...'

'What? I have to ask you?'

Aksel nodded. 'You have to ask me, because you already know what my answer will be. I'll wait.'

'You're very sure of yourself.'

'I'm very sure of *you*. And I'll be doing my best to wear you down...' He took her into his arms and kissed her. He'd answered none of her questions, but they were all irrelevant now. The only thing that mattered was that they loved each other.

'And how are you going to do that?'

He gave her a gorgeous grin. 'Close your eyes and imagine...'

Aksel wasn't sure whether he had a right to be this happy. But he'd take it. He'd stamped the fire out hastily, lucky not to singe his boots in the process, and he and Flora had hurried back down the hill. The only question that was left to ask was whether they'd spend the night in his bed or hers.

He reckoned that last night had to count towards the *wearing down* process. And then this morning, when they'd made love again, before rushing to work.

If Lyle noticed the coincidence of Aksel wanting to take Mette out after lunch and Flora asking for the afternoon off, he'd said nothing. The old SUV was now running smoothly and even though the outside left a little to be desired, it was now thoroughly clean inside and had a child seat in the back.

'Where are we going?' Flora felt as excited as Mette was.

'Wait and see.' Aksel took the road leading to the other side of the estate, through snow-covered grasslands, and then they bumped a little way across country to the half-acre plantation of Christmas trees. The larger ones, for the castle and the village marketplace had already been felled, but there were plenty of smaller ones that would fit nicely in Flora's cottage. He left Flora to help Mette out of the car seat, and opened the boot to retrieve the chainsaw he'd borrowed from Ted Mackie.

'No!' Flora clapped her hand over her mouth in horror when she saw him eyeing the plantation. 'We can't do that…isn't tree rustling some kind of crime?'

'I got permission from Charles. He says I can take whichever tree I want. Anyway, trees can't run away, so I'm sure it wouldn't technically be rustling.'

'Is it Christmas Eve tomorrow?' Mette started to jiggle up and down in excitement.

'In Scotland we can put up our tree as soon as we like, we don't have to wait until the day before Christmas Eve.'

Mette's eyes grew rounder. 'I *like* Scotland, Papa. Do we have *two* Christmases?'

'No, but there's Hogmanay.' Aksel grinned as Mette looked perplexed. 'You'll have to wait and see what that is.'

Mette nodded, and Aksel leaned towards Flora, her soft scent curling around him. 'I like Scotland, too.'

They took their time choosing, wandering through the plantation hand in hand, while

Mette relied on Kari to guide her through the snow. Mette declared that she wanted a tree tall enough for her to climb up to the sky, and Aksel explained that they couldn't get one like that into the cottage. In the end, Flora settled the argument by choosing one they all liked.

'Stand back...' He started up the chainsaw, grinning at Flora, and then cut a 'V' shape in the trunk. Flora hung tightly onto Mette's hand as she screamed excitedly. The tree fell exactly where Aksel had indicated it would.

He'd brought some netting, and Aksel wrapped the tree up in it, bending the larger branches upwards. Then he lifted the tree onto one shoulder to take it to the car. The raw power in his body never failed to thrill Flora. But there was more now. They were becoming a family.

'How long do I have to hold out for? Before I ask you to marry me?' Mette was busy scooping snow up to make a snowman, and Flora watched as Aksel loaded the tree into the car.

'Be strong.' He grinned at her. 'I'm finding that persuading you is much nicer than I'd thought. I have a few more things in mind.'

'What are they?'

'Breakfast in bed on Christmas morning. A Hogmanay kiss. Taking you back to Norway to meet my family after the New Year.'

Flora had always thought that the most romantic proposal must be a surprise. But planning it like this was even better than she'd dreamed. 'That sounds wonderful. Don't think that I won't be thinking of some things to persuade you.'

'So how long before we give in?' He leaned forward, growling the words into her ear as if they were a challenge.

'I think that decorating the tree's going to be the first big test of our resolve. Christmas Eve might prove very tempting...'

'Yes. That'll be difficult.' He took her hand, pulling off her glove and pressing her fingers to his lips.

'You'll be ready with your answer?' Flora smiled up at him.

'Oh, yes.' He wrapped his arms around her, kissing her. 'I'll be ready.'

EPILOGUE

Oslo, one year later

IT WAS THE night before Christmas Eve, and the family had gathered for Christmas. The big tree at Olaf and Agnetha's house was the centrepiece of the celebrations, and both Aksel's and Flora's parents were spending Christmas here this year. Everyone had admired the appliquéd Christmas stockings, a present from Mary Monroe, who had made a complete recovery and was back working at her beloved quilt shop three days a week.

Mette had fallen asleep as soon as her head had touched the pillow, and Aksel and Flora had tiptoed next door to their own room.

'Mum was telling me how welcome your parents have made her and Dad. They've been showing them around Oslo.' Flora slid onto the bed, propping herself up on the pillows next to Aksel, and he put his arm around her.

'I'm glad they get on so well. And with Olaf and Agnetha too.'

Flora nodded. 'I'm really going to miss this year. We did so much.'

They'd arranged a wedding and bought a house, one of the large stone-built properties just outside the village. Mette understood that her new family would always be there for her, and was gaining in confidence and exploring her world a little more each day. Aksel had been working at the canine therapy centre, after the previous vet had decided not to return from her maternity leave, and helping Ted Mackie organise adventure trips on the estate for the clinic's residents.

'I've got something to get us started on next year. I had an email from Charles this morning. He's signed the papers for the land, and it's now officially ours. We can start to build in the New Year.'

This had been Aksel's dream project, and Flora had fallen in love with it too. The small parcel of barren land, right on the edge of the estate, was no good for anything other than being ideally situated to build. Charles had sold it for a nominal amount, after Aksel had approached him with his plans for an adventure centre for people with disabilities.

'So it's a reality. That's fantastic!' Flora hugged him tight.

'Charles is as excited about it as I am. He offered to make a contribution towards the building costs, but I told him that if he wanted to do something, he could turn up and help dig out the foundations. He liked that idea much better.'

'I'm glad you decided that you weren't going to entirely give up on exploring. Even if these trips will be a little different.'

'They'll be even more challenging.' Aksel took her hand, pressing her fingers to his lips. 'And I'll never be away from my family for too long.'

'Well, maybe your family will just pack their bags every once in a while and come with you.'

He grinned. 'You know I'd love that.'

'I have something for you as well.' Flora

reached under the pillow, giving him the small, carefully wrapped package.

'Am I supposed to open this now?' He grinned at her.

'Yes.' She watched as he tore the paper, then turned the little fabric crocodile with sharp embroidered teeth over in his hands.

'All right. You've given me a crocodile to wrestle...?' He'd got the message and he was smiling at the thought of whatever challenge she was going to present him with now. 'Whatever it is you have in mind, the answer's yes.'

Flora nudged him in the ribs. 'You don't know what the question is yet.'

'It'll be Christmas Eve soon. And I trust you...'

It was his trust that had brought Flora to this point. They'd talked about this, and he'd told her that she'd know when the time was right. And she *did* know.

'You said that when we decided to start a family, we'd both take the test for the cystic fibrosis gene. Together...'

A broad grin spread across his face. He knew now exactly what she wanted.

'Yes. I did.'

'Are you ready, Aksel?'

He nodded. 'I've been ready for a long time. You?'

'I'm ready. If it turns out that we both carry the gene we have lots of options. Would it be irresponsible of me to say that we don't need to decide anything now? We'll know what to do if and when we find ourselves in that situation?'

'Nope. Life's one big exploration. You can't know what's ahead of you, but if you're travelling with someone you trust, you can be sure that you'll face it together.'

This felt like the first step in a journey that Flora couldn't wait to make. She kissed him, nestling into the warmth of his arms.

'So I'm going to be a dad again.' Aksel hugged her tight. 'I'm not going to miss a moment of it this time. I'll find someone else to lead the trips...'

'Whatever happens, it won't be for a little while. And when it does, you can have both, Aksel, you don't have to choose.' Sometimes she still had to remind him of that.

'How do you do it, Flora? Every time I think

that I'm about as happy as it's possible to be, you manage to make me happier.'

'Trust me Aksel. There's a lot more to come, for both of us.'

He laughed, pure joy spilling out of him. 'Oh, I trust you. Always.'

* * * * *

LET'S TALK
Romance

For exclusive extracts, competitions
and special offers, find us online:

f facebook.com/millsandboon

◎ @millsandboonuk

🐦 @millsandboon

Or get in touch on 0844 844 1351*

For all the latest titles coming soon,
visit millsandboon.co.uk/nextmonth